BLOOD & GUTS

VICKY DODDS BOOK 1

ED JAMES

ABOUT ED JAMES

Ed James writes crime-fiction novels, primarily the DI Simon Fenchurch series, set on the gritty streets of East London featuring a detective with little to lose. His Scott Cullen series features a young Edinburgh detective constable investigating crimes from the bottom rung of the career ladder he's desperate to climb.

Formerly an IT project manager, Ed began writing on planes, trains and automobiles to fill his weekly commute to London. He now writes full-time and lives in the Scottish Borders, with his girlfriend and a menagerie of rescued animals.

PROLOGUE

Christmas Eve, 2015

Teresa slalomed through the traffic lights, shooting along the road, the surface shining like glitter. She barrelled past the train station, for once not surrounded by roadworks, and passed the building site for that posh museum and that big old boat. The Discovery or something. They'd visited on a school trip and her mum and dad had taken her too, and she'd been *so* bored the first time, let alone the second.

Then the car jerked to the right and the steering wheel slipped through her fingers.

STEER INTO A SKID.

Her dad's advice rattled through her skull, so she fed

the wheel clockwise, like she was back in a driving lesson, scooping the hard plastic.

'Teri!' Carly rested her hand on the dashboard, like she was bracing for impact. 'Careful!'

'I *am* careful.' Teresa looked over at Carly in the passenger seat, all dolled up like she was going to a nightclub. Blonde hair trussed, waaaaaay too much make-up. But it worked for her. And Teresa was *so* jealous. Still, who was she to say *anyone* wasn't being careful? '*God*.'

'Just look ahead, aye?'

Teresa focused on the road, on her steering, faster than before. Who the hell was Carly bloody Johnston to criticise *her* driving? She hadn't even passed her test! Teresa didn't even slow at the roundabout by the hulking great Tesco, just slid round it.

'Teri, I swear to God...'

Teresa kept on along the road, a massive straight line, with just one pair of red rear lights up ahead. Nobody about, Christmas Eve quiet. Everyone tucked up at home, in bed or watching cheesy crap on the telly. Some lights hovered in the darkness over the river, a late train coming up from Edinburgh maybe.

Out of nowhere, a car battered out of the supermarket car parks, the wheels screeching as it fled away towards Perth.

'Jeez!' Carly was arching round, her mum's perfume

washing all over Teresa. She could taste it, that bitter tang that made her sneeze. 'Think he's robbed the place?'

Teresa slowed for this roundabout, indicating right and checking both other exits. 'Just a car dick making up for lost inches.'

Carly's throaty laugh echoed around her skull. '*Classic.*'

Teresa eased into the car park for the two supermarkets. Back the way they'd come. Tesco was the bigger of the two and still had a few punters walking around. Probably sad old men like Teresa's dad, out buying last-minute presents because they just didn't give a—

Nope.

He was in her head all the time already. Tonight, he was getting banished.

Teresa took the exit for the smaller supermarket. She used to come here with her dad when it was a DIY place, but now it was an Ashworth's. And there were hardly any cars, just a big empty lot of nothing. The store was long shut, the outside lights off, but people were still working inside in a dim glow.

It made her heart flutter.

Hayden would be out soon. He'd get in her car, and they'd drive off into the night, heading wherever they wanted for a few hours.

Carly was jerking her head around, hungry eyes scanning the car park, her frown growing in time with Teresa's slow progress down the lane. Then she smiled, probably the exact same smile as Teresa had on her face, but definitely for the same reason. Meeting her man. Carly clapped her hands then pointed to the side. 'There he is!'

One of those silver cars that *all* the taxi drivers used in Dundee. The engine was pluming exhaust into the dark night.

Teresa pulled up alongside, just a space between them. But the car looked empty. 'Where is he?'

The frown was back on Carly's forehead. 'I... I don't know.'

'The engine's running so he must be near.' Teresa kept looking over at the supermarket, trying to spot Hayden's casual stride, but the staff were all still inside. She grabbed her mobile from the cradle and there was a text:

Be another twenty minutes, babe.

Teresa felt herself shiver. The only good thing was it was sent ten minutes ago. Focus on the positives!

Carly's door was open and she was peering into her boyfriend's car. Still hadn't told anyone his name. God, such a drama queen.

Teresa got out into the freezing cold. All she had on was a dress – her fleece was in the boot – and it was sub-zero right now. Not that it would snow. No, they never got that lucky in Dundee. Soon as she was eighteen, she was out of here.

Carly was hugging her torso tight. 'There's nobody's here.'

'The boot's open.' Teresa shuffled forward, her heels clicking on the tarmac. 'Why would anyone leave it open like that?'

Carly crouched, cupping her hands on the glass to look inside.

A hand covered Teresa's mouth.

A bulky arm grabbed her from behind.

Someone whispered in her ear, 'Shhh.'

Then the hand went, but something still covered her mouth. Fabric maybe? A sleeve?

Was it Hayden playing a joke on her?

Pretty sick, even for him.

Would Carly's man do it? Before they'd even met?

Carly was playing with her phone, not even looking over. 'Where the *hell* is he?'

Something cold touched Teresa's neck. A knife! Someone had a knife on her!

She tried to scream but it was just a quiet moan. She tasted oily rag.

'Get in the boot.' She was lifted clean off her feet and dropped into the boot.

'Please!' But her words were all muffled.

The boot clicked shut and she was in darkness.

'What the hell?' Carly, outside.

'Help!' Teresa hit the inside of the boot, and the metal clattered. 'Help!'

Heels clicked off the tarmac outside. Carly running? Maybe.

Teresa thumped the boot again. Felt like something cracked in her hand.

She was trapped inside Carly's boyfriend's car. What the hell?

Someone shouted. A man's voice. She couldn't make it out. 'No. No, no, no.'

That was much clearer.

What the hell had happened?

A car door slammed. The car revved and shot off, pushing Teresa forward. Her head hit something hard.

1

Vicky lifted Bella up to look out of the window. Maybe they didn't live in the best part of Carnoustie, but at this time of year, with all the decorations and lights, it looked so lovely. Nothing too flashy or blinking or bling, just subtle and warm and friendly. 'Can you see Auntie Karen's car there?'

Bella tilted her wee head around, frowning. Her dark hair was getting pretty long, maybe time to cut it. Should've done that last week. Wouldn't get her into the hairdressers until after New Year, and even then, she'd squirm and wriggle and complain. And Vicky wouldn't be allowed to do it herself.

'No, Mummy. Where?'

She sighed, feeling a pang of pain in her heart, and pointed at the red Volvo with 13 plates. 'Zulu, alpha, 13.

Sierra, Juliet, Bravo.' God, she needed to turn off the police part of her brain for a few days. 'See?'

A hand was waving through the windscreen.

'Oh! There she is, Mummy!' Bella waved back.

'Come on, Bells.' Vicky hefted her back down onto the floor. 'Let's go and see her.' She grabbed Bella's tiny hand and led her through the living room, with that massive tree Bella wanted sitting in the corner. That area underneath was still free for "Santa" to ram full of wrapped presents later, not that the little minx would go to bed until late.

Karen was at the front door, misting the glass with her breath and drawing a love heart.

Vicky opened the door. 'Hey, Karen.'

'Evening, ladies.' Karen swooped Bella up in her arms. 'How's my little princess?' She carried Bella through to the living room.

Vicky stepped outside and picked up the massive box sitting on the step. A doll's house wrapped and just small enough for her to carry it herself. Karen's daughter's friend's mum's sister's old one, but the kid was at high school now, so it was an absolute steal. Vicky shuffled it into the porch and nudged the door shut with her hip.

A wail of giggles erupted from the living room.

Now.

Vicky grabbed the box and lugged it up the stairs, thumping on each one, but the giggles and squeals got even louder. The plan was working to perfection. She got it into her bedroom and dropped it on the far side of her bed. Chest heaving. Christ, she needed to get running again. Chance would be a fine thing.

All of Bella's presents were under the bed, ready for Santa to work his magic once the wee beastie had gone to bed.

Vicky took a deep breath, her heart rate back under control, then shut her bedroom door and set off down the stairs.

Karen and Bella were on the sofa, opposite the TV mounted above the fireplace. Not quite at the right angle, thanks to her dad and her brother's half-arsed attempts and stupid arguments.

Vicky collapsed into the armchair. 'Can I get you a drink, Kaz?'

'Thought you'd never ask.'

'Wine?'

'White.'

'White? Christ.' Vicky raised her eyebrows. 'You'll be smashing the place up before Bella's gone to bed.'

'I'm not that bad, am I?'

'No, but you're not that good.' Vicky heaved herself up and padded through to the kitchen. The bottle of white looked sad in the fridge, filled with kids' treats, salads and not much else. She poured out two glasses and took them back through, just as *that song* blasted out of the speakers.

Bella had already got her way, getting Karen to put *Frozen* on. Not that it was ever out of the DVD player.

'I see she's already asked.' Vicky handed Karen the glass. 'And you've already agreed.'

'I'm a soft touch, Vicks.' Karen sniffed her glass, but it was like she was sucking in the aroma rather than testing it for freshness, though she had been known to sometimes do subtle. 'Colin's the one who does all the hard stuff in our house.'

'He's not working tonight, then?'

'No. He's looking after kids. New neighbour a few weeks ago. He's coming in for some wine, letting his boy play with our two.' Karen looked up from her glass. 'Should maybe have invited you over. He's hot.'

'Kaz...'

'Seriously, Vicks. Don't you thi—'

Vicky's smile cut her off. 'Maybe after she's gone to bed.'

'Okay.' Karen rubbed Bella's hair. 'Just that she could've had some friends tonight, that's all.'

'Well, we've been saying we needed a girlie night for a while. My brother's got me *Top Gun* and *Dirty Dancing* and—'

'*Top Gun*. No question.'

Vicky raised her glass to her lips and tasted the sweet wine.

Just as her mobile rang.

Vicky put her glass down on the side table. 'Who's that?'

Karen shrugged. 'Ignore it.'

'It might be Mum...'

'You're round there tomorrow, aye?'

'Christmas with the Doddses.' Vicky picked up her mobile just as it stopped ringing.

There was a missed call and a text she hadn't heard. From Alan. Christ – she thought she'd blocked his number. Vicky switched the bloody thing off, then picked up her glass again. Trying to focus on the here and now, not the there and then.

Karen was looking over with that nosy glint in her eyes. 'Who's that?'

'My brother.' Vicky felt the lie turn into a blush on her neck, but it was only a white one – one day, she'd be able to talk to Karen about Alan, about everything that had happened, but that wasn't today. 'Daft sod.'

'You're back in touch with him, then?'

'Just through Mum and Dad. Well, just Mum really. He's back living there, but he isn't well.'

'In a—'

Now the house phone rang.

'Christ, I've got to take it, don't I?' Vicky got up and charged through to the hall. That retro phone seemed like a cool idea in the shop, but the practicalities of a rotary dial in the age of mobile phones wasn't exactly as good as a cheapo cordless, though the actual bell-ringing sound was nice. She picked it up. 'Hello?'

'Doddsy, it's David.'

DI David Forrester, and it wasn't likely that he'd be wishing her a happy Christmas, when it comes.

'What's up, sir?'

Forrester coughed. 'Just wondering if you'd heard from DS Ennis.'

'Ryan?' Vicky frowned. 'Not for a couple of days since I went off on leave. Why?'

'Well, he's supposed to be on shift, only I can't get hold of the bugger. A lassie's been killed.'

Vicky shut her eyes. 'Is this you saying you need me to come in?'

Another cough. 'Would you be able to?'

Vicky exhaled. She wasn't allowed to put herself first for one night, even after eighteen consecutive days at work... 'Okay, I'll get Mum to come round to babysit Bella.'

'And if you know where Karen Woods is?'

2

An hour later, but it looked like a year's worth of activity had taken place.

Vicky slowed, her window whirring down, and she held out her ID. 'Evening, Dumpy.'

'Sarge.' The tall male uniformed officer manning the entrance filled out the form for her. He was a good example of why the police could do with a maximum height, as he must have to stoop to get through every doorway. 'DS Vicky Dodds and DC Karen Woods.' He gave a curt nod. 'DI Forrester is in the inner locus.'

'Thanks.' Vicky navigated her car across the icy car park, shiny sparkles rather than the sheer hell that was black ice.

The brutal supermarket lurked in the background, a dim outline behind the bright glow of the arc lights. Even the Ashworth's sign was dulled, probably the only time of year it would be, Christmas and New Year – even Easter was a major shopping holiday now.

She parked as near as she could, but it wasn't exactly right by the store. A few cars were huddled closer, must be for staff. Inside the front door, more uniformed cops interviewed frustrated workers, all looking outside and no doubt asking when they could go. But maybe someone had seen something. Maybe.

'Can still taste that wine.' Karen ran her tongue over her lips. 'Not like you to get good stuff in.'

'Well, it is Christmas, isn't it?' Vicky opened her door and got out into the bitter night. She set off towards the crime scene, wrapping her coat tight around her.

For once, the entrance to the glowing white tent wasn't flapping in a breeze. Even this close to the Tay, it was perfectly still.

Karen got to the inner locus first and grabbed the clipboard to sign them in. 'DI Forrester around?'

DC Stephen Considine was all suited up, his tangerine hair bright through the translucent hood. Still had acne despite being late twenties, if a day. Not quite tall enough to be the barrier his body language made him out to be. He thumbed behind him, but he seemed more interested in the cars parked nearby, especially a white BMW. 'Aye, the gaffer's inside.'

Karen handed the clipboard back with a nod. 'Thanks.' She tossed a crime scene suit towards Vicky.

She caught it just as the tent flap opened wide.

The unmistakeable hunched figure of Forrester stomped out, shaking his head and snarling through his mask. 'I don't bloody care.'

Trailing behind was the source of his ire. Vampish red hair a few shades darker than Considine's crowded Jenny Morgan's mask, but her icy smile seemed to make the air even colder. 'I don't bloody care if you don't bloody care, David. It's Christmas Eve and—'

'And you've got a teenage lassie found half-clothed and dead in a supermarket car park.' Forrester stopped, maybe letting his point sink in. 'I don't give—'

'Look, I hate Christmas as much as the next Satanist, but my staff aren't so enlightened.'

'Well, I don't give a monkey's what day it is. That lassie has parents and a killer. If I'm to tell the former that I can't catch the latter because you can't manage your team? Christmas is cancelled. If your lot want a job that guarantees them off tonight, I suggest they inquire at Ashworth's.'

'Fine.' Jenny's snort looked like she was anything but. Still, she followed it with a resigned sigh, then a nod. 'Evening, Vicks. Getting your evening ruined too?'

Vicky gave a warm smile, trying to disarm Jenny on behalf of Forrester, but it didn't seem to cut the mustard. 'I'm hoping you'd have solved the case before I got here.'

'Nah, that's your job, Vicks.' Jenny stepped aside and started tearing at her crime scene suit. Her phone rang and she answered it, trousers around her ankles.

Inside the tent, Vicky saw the familiar sight of Dr Shirley Arbuthnott's massive backside squatting by a body, side on to Vicky in a patch of petrol almost in the middle of a parking space. Looked like a teenager dressed for clubbing. A baby-blue dress that barely touched her thighs. Matching heels, though one had been discarded. Her lifeless eyes stared this way. Hard to see the cause of death this far away, just looked like the kind of prank kids would get up to on social media. That new Instagram thing, maybe. Or a video on YouTube. But the victim looked young, barely sixteen.

Time was, that would've been Vicky, dressed up for a night on the town. In years to come, it could be Bella. A shiver crawled up her spine, like the cold had got deep into her bones.

Jenny stabbed a finger off her phone and kicked the crime scene suit trousers up in the air. 'Jay's found a Samsung smartphone nearby.' She caught the trousers and dumped them on the discard pile. 'I'm going to head back to the station to work at it.'

Forrester scowled at her. 'I need you here, though.'

'No, you don't.' Jenny smiled. 'You need *my team* here, working on any forensics, not me. And there won't be any, will there?' She looked around. 'Meanwhile, I'm going to get into that phone and see who your girl was meeting.'

'Meeting?'

'Well, you don't come here dressed like that if you're out for a stroll, do you?'

'You're assuming she wasn't dumped?'

'Same difference. She's probably been speaking to her killer. Happens all the time.'

Forrester looked desperate now, his eyes darting around the car park. 'Are you cataloguing the cars?'

'Not my job, David. You've got a very big team who can handle that kind of malarkey.'

Forrester shut his eyes. 'Right. Well. Off you bloody go.'

'Charming.' Jenny patted Vicky's arm as she passed. 'Catch you guys later.'

Forrester nodded at Karen. 'Constable, see that stuff about cataloguing cars?'

'Can't you get DC Considine to do it?'

Forrester frowned, but it eased off when he spotted Considine's eager bunny nodding. 'Aye, fine. Relieve him from Crime Scene Management.'

'Thanks, sir.'

Forrester watched them go, easing off his suit trousers. 'Swear she gets worse every day, Vicks.'

'Karen or Jenny?'

'Take your pick.'

The tent opened and Arbuthnott stormed out, lugging her medicine bag. 'Well, David, I'll check to see if she was raped when I get her back.'

Vicky felt like her gut was boiling now. 'Raped?'

'It's possible.' Arbuthnott grimaced. 'Sooner I get her into the lab, the sooner—'

'But if you were a betting lady?'

Arbuthnott exhaled slowly, her breath misting in the air. 'My take is that the victim was strangled and then dumped here.'

Vicky looked around the car park again. 'Why would you dump a body here?'

'Good question.' Arbuthnott shrugged. 'But the body's still warm, so I can give you a very accurate time of death.' She checked her watch. 'Eighty-two minutes ago.'

Forrester gave her a warmer smile than he gave Jenny. 'Any danger we can get the PM fast tracked?'

Arbuthnott was nodding her head. 'I mean, it's Christmas Eve and all of my children are waiting on Santa's visit, but this is a young girl's life, snuffed out just like that.' She clicked her fingers. 'As soon as she's in the mortuary, I'll fast-track a preliminary post-mortem.'

'I appreciate it, Shirley.'

'I'm not the one who has to break the news to her parents. Evening.' Arbuthnott hefted up her bag again and charged across the car park.

Vicky stood there, trying to process it all. A dead girl

in the middle of a supermarket car park. 'Take it we don't know who she is?'

'No purse, no ID. Nothing.' Forrester folded up his trousers and put them on the discard pile. 'Hoping that, despite her general nippiness, Jenny can get us at least that from the phone.'

'Assuming it's the victim's.'

'Right.'

'Who found the body?'

'Night security lad.' Forrester was scratching at his seven o'clock shadow, rasping like a matchbox. 'Lad wasn't the full shilling. More excited about how he's working all of Christmas Day too and how he's coining it in at double time. Some nonsense about going to Barcelona in a week to watch the El Clásico and tour the stadium.'

'David, "the" is redundant.'

'Eh?'

'It's El Clásico, not *the* El Clásico.'

'Either way, I fancy Barca crushing Real.'

'Displacement activity, right?' Vicky looked over at the supermarket, now emptying of staff. 'He's just found a dead body. Can't process that, so he talks about football.'

'Right.'

She focused on him. 'Unless he killed her.'

'Already crossed my mind.' Forrester shot her a crafty wink, just the wrong side of creepy. 'Lad didn't see anybody turn up, though.'

'You believe him?'

'I do. Young Buchan got hold of the CCTV.' Forrester pulled out a smartphone and pressed his finger to the sensor. 'Bastard thing never— Here we go.' He held out the screen to Vicky.

It was paused, showing a car driving over from the roundabout. A silver Skoda, but blurry. Vicky nudged the frame on but it disappeared. Back two, and it was over at the roundabout.

Forrester scowled. 'They've got the world's worst security system.'

'It's 2015 – who only stores every five seconds?'

'Ashworth's is who. Cheap bastards.' Forrester shook his head. 'Had a case over at their head office in Crieff a few years back. Bunch of clowns, I tell you. Had to threaten both brothers. Twins, would you believe?'

'Believe anything. So, you think this Skoda dumped her body here?'

'Possible.' He took the phone back and held it out, on the frame of the car. 'You see both of our problems, though, aye?'

Vicky stared at the screen, but she couldn't see much else. Ah. She had it. 'So, there's no CCTV nearer the store?'

'Nope. It's like Fort Knox, Doddsy.' Forrester shook his head. 'Cameras everywhere. And in glorious HD. Just not out there. Not their land, so no dice on the old cameras.'

'And that car doesn't show up?'

'Correct.'

Vicky stared at the screen again. 'No, I don't see what the issues are.'

Forrester tapped the screen. 'The car's got masked plates.'

'That's not just blur?'

'No, that Jay gadgie in forensics ran it through his laptop, said it's been sprayed with that shite that, you know, *masks* it.'

'It's a Skoda, right?'

'Right. An Octavia. Why?'

'Well, my dad's always joking about how—'

'All taxis in Dundee are Skoda Octavias. Aye.'

'What's the other one?'

'Well, if that car didn't dump her, then let's say they were meeting here. We've got one other car coming and —' Forrester's frown deepened into a scowl. 'In the name of the wee man...' He powered off across the car park. 'Shite!' He slid forward, arms rising, but at least he didn't go down.

Vicky followed him, but slowly. 'Watch for the ice, sir.'

'Aye, aye.' But Forrester wasn't to be deterred. 'Ryan!'

A car door opened and a tall bugger got out, his face obscured by a thick beard. His bald head caught the light. DS Ryan Ennis was weaving about, like he was drunk. 'Eh?'

Vicky felt her gut clench in that sickening way. Christ knows how Ennis did what he did to her, but he did it.

'Been trying to bloody call you!' Forrester held out his phone, emphasising his point. 'I've texted, I've left voice-mails! Where the hell have you been?'

Ennis leaned back against his car and folded his arms. 'Daughter's run off *again*. Took her granda's car. Suspect she's seeing her boyfriend, but I've no bloody idea who he is. Neither does Kelly. And I'm *raging*.' He didn't seem to be anything like raging. Just stood there, with the same dead expression on his face. He looked over at Vicky and his eyes twinkled with mischief. 'Vicks. Just you wait until wee Bella's seventeen, then you'll see.'

Vicky clenched her jaw tight.

Before she could say anything, Forrester was in Ennis's face. 'You've got a bloody cheek. Can't get hold of your daughter and *you're* raging? Why aren't you at least doing me the courtesy of letting me know you'd gone off duty? Eh?'

Ennis sniffed, eyes shut. 'Sorry, Dave.'

'Don't "Dave" me. This is serious. A lassie's been killed and—'

'Said I'm sorry.'

Forrester stood there, his tongue worming around in his cheek. Vicky knew that look. Trying to figure out how much punishment to mete out.

'Wait a wee minute.' Ennis shot into action, charging

across the car park like a bull driving at a matador, his heavy feet pounding away.

While he was distracted by Ennis's appearance and equally sudden disappearance, Vicky nudged Forrester's arm. 'Sir, now he's turned up, do you mind if me and Karen can get off home?'

'Give me a bloody minute!' Forrester started off after Ennis.

As much as Vicky wanted to get home, this kind of drama needed to be sorted out. And Ennis was prone to worse. So she followed too.

Ennis had a hold of Considine's suit lapels and had pulled him close. 'Of course I do, you arsehole!' Ennis looked like he was going to chin him.

Forrester was trying to prise him off. 'What the bloody hell is going on?'

'This big wanker—'

'You, son, are a useless wee fanny.' Ennis took a step forward, head jutting out towards Considine, but he stopped short of sticking the head on him. 'How could you *not know*?'

Forrester got some traction and hauled Ennis away from Considine. 'Know what, Ryan?'

Ennis stood there, head darting around. 'The car.' His shaking hand was pointing at a battered old Peugeot that surely couldn't be roadworthy. Bruise purple, with lichen or moss growing in the radiator. 'It's...' He took a deep breath. 'It's my wife's father's car.'

Forrester frowned. 'Does he work here?'

Ennis shook his head. 'My... daughter uses it to ferry the old bugger around. Teresa... She's...' He barged past Forrester, then set off into a jog, then as close to a sprint as his giant frame could manage. 'Teri!'

He was heading for the crime scene.

Vicky raced off after him, but he was at the tent before she was halfway there. And Karen was no match for his bulk, half his weight. At least. But she had a baton extended, raised behind her back, saying something lost to Ennis's manic shouting.

Vicky grabbed his arm and pulled him back.

The ice was on her side and he slipped and slid towards her. 'That's my daughter in there!'

Vicky kept hold of his arm. 'We'll show you a photo, okay?'

'Fine.'

Karen kept a glare fixed on Ennis, ready to smash him with her baton.

Vicky walked over to the crime scene tent. 'Jen, can you show us a photo?'

Jenny peered out, holding a tablet computer. 'Here.'

'Cheers.' Vicky held it out to Ennis. 'Is this her?'

Panting hard, Ennis stared at the screen, mouth hanging open. He collapsed into Vicky's arms.

She let two of the bigger nearby uniforms take him, then stared into his eyes. 'Ryan, is it Teresa?'

Ennis shook his head. 'No. It's not.'

'Do you recognise—?'

'Why the bloody hell is her car here?'

Vicky grabbed his lapels now. 'Ryan, do you recognise her?'

Ennis looked right at her, then nodded slowly. 'Aye. Aye, I do. She's... She's a friend of Teresa's. Name is Carly Johnston.'

3

A delaide Place was a long street filled with big old houses just that bit too close together. The Johnstons' home was one of the more spread out, and had a great view down to the Tay, with both bridges glowing in the freezing fog.

Vicky turned to face Forrester, silhouetted by the lights of Dundee behind him, stretching down the Law to the pitch-black Tay. On a night like this, it almost felt like a safe place. '*Hate* doing this.'

Forrester looked up from his phone, the brightness catching his face. 'What, interrupting a pleasant dinner party to tell parents their pride and joy has been killed and maybe raped?' He let out a thick sigh. 'Aye, it's shite.'

Vicky rang the bell and let it chime. Inside the house, soft jazz played from somewhere, accompanied by laughing and joking. Some kind of party, or maybe just watching a film at ear-splitting volume. She stepped back, clasping her hands around her back. She didn't know what to do with them, where to put her fingers, now squirming against her palms.

Forrester clicked his jaw, in that really sickening way. 'Poor Ryan.'

Vicky nodded.

Still, nobody was answering.

Forrester stepped forward and rapped his knuckles on the door, that stern policeman's pattern that never failed.

'Poor lad didn't take being sent back to the station too well.'

Vicky clenched her hands into fists. 'I think you should've sent him home.'

'Eh?' Forrester shook his head. 'Him remaining in the station means he's close to any news. Professional courtesy, if nothing else. Besides, if I sent him home, you know he'll somehow not turn up there and be out looking for what the hell's happened to Teresa.'

Vicky gave him as polite a nod as she could muster.

So much for Forrester's policeman's knock. She reached over to press the bell again. 'Still think he's a powder keg waiting to explode.'

'Aye, well, I can handle Ryan Ennis.'

'Sure. That's why you had to drag me in on Christmas Eve.'

'Come on, Vicky, it's a man thing.'

'A *man* thing?'

'Aye. I can't just send him away. He's—'

The door clunked open, replaced by a man with rosy cheeks. Mid-forties, short hair, his smart shirt open at the neck to reveal a wiry chest rug. He tilted his head to the side. 'Can I help you?'

'Name's David Forrester. This is my colleague, Vicky Dodds. I'm a detective inspector in Pol—'

'What's happened?'

Forrester paused. 'It's best we do this inside, sir.'

'Is it Carly?'

'Sir, I sugg—'

'Is she okay?'

'Bill, what's going on?' A woman appeared, clinging to his arm. 'What's happened?'

Forrester had his warrant card out. 'We just need a word inside. About your daughter.'

'My God. Is she okay?'

Forrester closed his eyes and gave a grimace. He clearly knew he wasn't getting inside. 'I'm afraid the body of someone matching her description was found this evening. We'll need one of you to identify her.'

'A HELL of a time to do this, Vicky.' Forrester rested his hand against the wall, like he was bracing himself against the news. 'Every bloody Christmas Eve for the rest of their lives, they'll be scarred by losing their daughter.'

Through the thick safety glass, Arbuthnott pulled back the sheet to show the victim's face. On the edge of being a girl and a woman. Whatever had led her to that fate, dying in a cold supermarket car park, maybe it had something to do with her exploring what becoming a woman meant.

Or maybe it had nothing to do with it.

Vicky stepped closer to the glass to get a better look at what was going on.

Bill and Catherine Johnston stood in the room next to Arbuthnott, holding hands, faces stern in that Dundonian way, but his eyes and her lips betrayed their grief.

Bill gave Arbuthnott the nod, and she replaced the sheet with a kind smile. Arbuthnott glanced at the window, then led the Johnstons away.

Forrester ran a hand down his face. 'Hell of a time.' He walked off himself, heading for the family room, but stopped by the door. 'Here's the deal, okay? I'll babysit the parents for a bit, stay for the PM, see if I can shake anything loose. Arbuthnott's readying her just now.' He grimaced. 'You get back to the team, see what you can divine.'

'Deal.' Vicky lingered in the empty room, staring at

the body under the sheet. Not yet autopsied, but identified now at least. Carly Johnston, her future snuffed out in a single moment. Christ, it didn't bear thinking about.

She walked over to the door, catching it as it swung shut, then entered the family room.

'But you will catch them, aye?' Bill Johnston wasn't letting Forrester go, just drilling his gaze deep into his eyes.

'We will try, sir. Yes, of course we will.' Forrester sat at the table opposite the Johnstons' sofa. 'Can I get you a tea or a coffee?'

'You can *get* the animal who murdered my daughter.' Johnston's voice was low, but full of venom. Betrayed his profession, just like any high school teacher might in this situation.

'We're determined to identify all of the events surrounding your daughter's death, sir.' Forrester shook free, then sat on the cheap armchair, his hands splayed on his lap. 'Do you know where she was going this evening?'

Bill crumpled, his face falling. He slumped into the sofa next to his wife, who was intent on staring at the floor. 'Well, we were having friends over for dinner. Kind of a... a tradition, and... and Carly was... She was out for the evening.' He looked over at Forrester with a steely glint. 'Do you have children?'

'Two boys.'

Then he stared at Vicky. 'And you?'

'A daughter. She's three.'

'Right. Well. You've got it all to come.'

Vicky nodded in sympathy. 'Did Carly have a boyfriend?'

'Not that we know of.' Bill sniffed. 'As far as we knew, she was going to a friend's house to watch a film.'

Forrester glanced over at the door, briefly locking eyes with Vicky. 'You got a name for this friend?'

Bill frowned at his wife.

She nodded at Forrester. 'It was Ashley. Ashley Mitchell. Her parents were the ones over for dinner.'

Vicky felt something tighten in her gut. This didn't explain why Teresa Ennis's car was there. 'Does she know a Teresa Ennis?'

'Well, I think she's in her class.' Catherine looked over at her husband. 'But I wasn't aware they were friends. Why?'

'A car belonging to Miss Ennis's grandfather was found at the scene.'

'I see.' Catherine blew out air. 'Well.'

Vicky waited for eye contact, which didn't take long. The desperate searching gaze of a grieving mother, looking for answers as much as the father was looking for vengeance. 'Do you have an address for Ashley Mitchell?'

4

'This is what we've got to look forward to.' Karen got out of the car first.

Vicky followed her out into the cold air. 'Right.'

A deep thud came from somewhere, the slow and steady thump of dance music. The calendar might move on every year, but the kids never changed – when mum and dad were away, the kids will get absolutely shit-faced and put on shit dance music.

Same street as the Johnstons' home, and similarly upmarket, but jammed between two older homes. A small front garden, but an oak tree towered over the house from the back, all lit up from below. Strobe lights flashed inside, like someone was having an illegal rave.

Karen set off towards the front door. 'Doubt we'll be

the first officers round here tonight.' She thumbed the bell. The modern tone was shriller than the pleasant tone of the Johnstons'.

'Maybe they'll take notice of us, though.' Vicky scanned the street. 'Wonder where the parents are?'

'What, because you broke up their little gathering?'

'Right. I mean, it's not exactly far away, is it? Why has it taken them this long to get back here?'

'Maybe they're waiting for Carly's parents? That whole moral support thing?'

'Maybe.' Vicky peered in the front window. Dark inside, and hard to make anyone out in the flickering strobe, but the music cut from house music to something Vicky hadn't heard in a long time. '*Poison*. The Prodigy. Christ, that takes me back.'

Kids started jumping around inside the room, shouting 'Ya!' in time with the record.

'Bugger it.' Karen tried the door handle, and it opened wide, the music bleeding into the reeking smell of cannabis. 'Christ, the parents are only a few doors away, not in Spain.' She stepped inside and cupped her hands around her mouth. 'Police!'

The music stopped dead and the kids all looked around, the nearest girl's mouth forming a shocked O. She looked about twenty, older than the others.

Vicky charged over and grabbed her arm before she could flee. 'We're looking for Ashley Mitchell.'

She frowned. 'That's me. What have I done?'

'Do your parents know about this?'

Ashley shrugged. 'They're cool with it. Out at some lame-ass dinner party.'

Vicky checked around the room again. Karen was doing a good job of blocking the door and stopping anyone leaving. A lot of drunk teenagers, hiding behind the dining table covered in DJ equipment. The mixmaster himself looked about forty, though.

Vicky focused on Ashley again. 'Aren't you a bit old for this crowd?'

'What? I'm sixteen.'

'Right.' Vicky wasn't sure that was true. 'We're looking for Carly Johnston and Teresa Ennis.'

'Very pleased for you.'

'It's a serious matter.'

'So?'

'So, Ashley, you need to talk to me.'

'Free country.'

'Even freedom has its limits.' Vicky held her gaze, and it was much harder than it should be with the blonde fringe covering Ashley's eyes. 'Especially as Carly's body was found this evening.'

The O returned to her lips. 'What?'

'This isn't about your party, Ashley, but your parents will probably be here soon, so you should get this lot packed away.'

'Right.' Ashley waved over at the middle-aged super-star DJ. 'Kenny, can you—?'

'Aye, aye.' His voice was a fractured squeak.

Ashley led Vicky away from the throng towards a warm-looking kitchen. A young couple snogged by the window and didn't pay much attention to anything except each other's underwear. 'Okay, were Carly and Teri here?'

Ashley let out a sigh. 'Aye, they were. But for like five minutes. Too cool for this kind of thing.'

'Know where they went?'

'Think they went to meet their boyfriends?'

A statement voiced as a question. Did that mean she was more or less likely to be telling the truth?

'Do you know where?'

'Sorry, but they're like really stuck up?'

'Did Carly or Teri ever talk about their boyfriends?'

'Look, I don't know what you think is going on.'

'Your parents were at Carly's house. Aren't you close?'

'Carly ain't my friend.' Ashley rolled her eyes at them. 'We used to be, but she, like, thinks she's better than us.'

'Right. I totally get that.'

'I mean, Teri is good people.' Jesus, all these Americanisms. Dundonian slang will be a lost art soon enough. 'She sits next to me in English.'

'And did Teri ever talk about any boyfriends?'

'Like, I think so.' Ashley's eyes darted around the

room. 'But I don't know.' She frowned. 'Carly's really dead.' Her questions were like statements.

Vicky nodded. 'Her parents just identified her.'

'What happened.'

'We just need to speak to her boyfriend.'

The couple in the corner broke off from their snog. The boy – tall and skinny – was smirking. 'Isn't it Gary?'

'Shut up, Josh?' Ashley shook her head at him. 'And get out of here! She's a narc.'

Josh and his dark-haired lover darted out of the room.

Vicky settled her gaze on Ashley. 'I'm not a fed.'

'You are?'

'No, I'm a police officer.'

'Same difference.'

'Ashley, who is Gary?'

She rolled her eyes again. 'Josh is such a douchebag. Why did he have to do that?'

'Okay, but you know who Gary is?'

Still shaking her head, Ashley pointed into a big dining room extension. 'He's in there.'

'Thank you.' Vicky walked back into the hall and spotted Karen, still guarding the door, and got the thumbs up. Not her first rodeo, by any stretch. Vicky turned and entered the dining room, still with that smell of fresh paint.

A few kids sat around a dining table playing poker and smoking a cigar. A cigar that smelled funny. What did they call it when they hollowed a cigar out and replaced it with marijuana?

Great, these kids thought they were rappers.

'Put the...' oh yeah, '...blunt down.' Vicky stood at the head of the table. 'Which one of you is Gary?'

The kids were barely sixteen, but were trying to look and act like adults. They left their cards face down, poker chips in the middle of the table, and all got up.

The one with the blunt rested it on the edge of a can of Hooch alcoholic lemonade and pointed to the back of the room. 'That's him.' He shot off after his mates.

Someone was shouting, 'It's the pigs!' Through the house, doors slammed, kids shouted and thundered down the staircase.

Karen had lost the battle.

This room looked out onto a well-kept but narrow garden, pebbles spread out around flower beds, some mature trees with benches, and the giant oak at the back with a swing on it. Only one pair of kids had braved the elements to sit on the swing and kiss. Probably so pissed they weren't aware of the police presence.

A lone kid was watching them, hand pressed against the glass. Dark hair down to his shoulder, greasy and something he could hide behind. He held a box of red wine, swigging from the nozzle.

'Gary?'

He turned around to look at Vicky, frowning and

completely off his face. Eyes rolling, mouth hanging open. 'Huh?'

'Are you Gary?'

'Depends.' He burped, long and loud. 'Who's asking.'

'Detective Sergeant Vicky Dodds.' She held out her warrant card.

'Right.' Either he was too far gone to notice he was talking to a cop, or he didn't care. Maybe both.

'GET OUT!' a man's voice bellowed through the house. 'GET THE HELL OUT OF HERE!'

Ashley was cowering in the middle of the hallway, as a bear-like man shouted and tried to punch passing kids. The DJ had his gear all boxed up, but he couldn't get past the man.

'Kenny? What the *hell* are you doing here?'

'Sorry, Scott.' And Kenny swerved past him.

Presumably Scott was Ashley's father, Carly's parents' dinner date.

Karen approached him, warrant card out, and that only seemed to spark his rage.

Vicky turned back to Gary.

But he was gone – just an empty box of wine on the floor.

The French doors slammed and Gary was scarpering across the pebbles.

Just great.

Vicky jerked into action, tearing the door open and crunching across the icy pebbles towards him.

Gary was hurtling towards the couple on the swing, who only noticed him as he reached them, then he used them as a stepping stone to climb up the oak.

'Police!' Vicky stopped at the bottom of the tree. 'Get down!'

The couple fled back towards the house, both shrieking.

Vicky looked up the tree, at the translucent green soles of Gary's Dr. Martens. All she could think of was that Edinburgh cop she'd spoken to on a training course, big lump who'd chased a cat up a tree and got no end of abuse for it from his peers, even after rescuing the poor moggy. Vicky had absolutely no idea how to get up there.

But she needed to – one of the branches hung over the wall and the drunk little sod was heading for it.

No, she needed another option. Wait. She reached into her belt and got out her baton. 'Gary, I will throw this at you. It will hurt. A lot.'

He turned to look down at her. But it stopped his progress towards the brick wall, maybe a metre away, almost close enough to jump.

She held her baton behind her head, like she did back at school when throwing the javelin.

'Wait!' He held up a hand. 'Wait!' A loud hiccup, like he'd downed a box of air as well as the wine.

She lowered her baton.

Just as he lost his footing on the tree, slipping down the rough bark.

Vicky jolted forward and held out her arms. She caught him, but he was too heavy and took her down too. She thumped her head against the bark, and it felt like she'd opened her skull. Somehow she got a tight grip on the kid's arm. 'Stop!'

He looked around at her, his mouth even wider than Ashley's had been moments earlier. But he'd lost all the fight, all the piss and vinegar. He just hiccupped.

Vicky felt her temple, but somehow had avoided any blood. The wound was just agony. Probably get a nice Christmas bruise. She grabbed him under the armpits, hot and sweaty, and pulled him up to standing. 'Gary, stop resisting me.'

He was hiding behind his lank hair again. 'What do you want?'

'I need to speak to you about Carly Johnston.'

'Why?'

Before Vicky could answer, Gary jerked forward and sprayed second-hand red wine all over his boots.

5

Despite the pair of trainers from Lost Property, Gary still reeked of red wine and stomach acid.

Vicky couldn't decide which was worse.

And he was just a kid. Looked so young, younger than anyone at that party. But he had a haunted look about him too, backed up with tanning a box of cheap wine. That was a fast way to oblivion. Hard to decide if his look was contrived, or if it betrayed some deep trauma. Could be both, or it could just be how he was born, the shape of his sharp cheekbones.

Vicky leaned across the table and tried to direct her voice at the microphone. 'Gary, it'll be better for you if you talk to us.'

But he couldn't bring himself to look at her. Eyes

closed. Taking deep breaths. At least he'd stopped hiccupping, though the duty doctor couldn't give any reassurances that he wasn't going to be sick again. And just under the blood alcohol level – the purging of his guts had a beneficial side to it.

'Gary, seriously. We're speaking to you in relation to a murder inquiry.'

He just shook his head. Still couldn't look at her.

'Carly's dead.'

Even that didn't work. Gary just flared his nostrils. At least his eyes were open now.

Vicky caught a look from Karen, one that read "what the hell is this kid on?" Vicky leaned forward again, close enough to smell the second-hand booze wafting off him. She widened her eyes, trying to emphasise how deep in the shite he was. 'Someone found her dead body, Gary.'

More head shaking.

'You do know her, right?'

He swallowed.

'Were you her boyfriend?'

The shaking got faster. He pursed his lips. But still he didn't speak.

'Someone told us you were her boyfriend.'

'Someone should shut their mouth.'

Vicky sat back, pleased to get a response from him. 'When I identified myself as a police officer, you ran away. Is that because you killed her?'

'What?' Staring at the floor now.

'Because that seems like the kind of thing a guilty person would do.'

'I haven't— I...' He let out a monster sigh that seemed to take all of his energy. 'I haven't done anything.'

'Sure? Where were you heading?'

'Nowhere.'

'Sure about that? Because it looked like you were heading for that wall. Someone else's garden, then out onto the street and you could get away. Right?'

'I just needed to climb.'

'Come on, you've got to do better than that.'

Gary sat back, arms folded, that haunted look in full effect. '*Knew* I shouldn't have gone.'

Okay, so he was talking. Vicky wanted to keep him like that. 'Why not, Gary?'

'Because.'

'Who were you there with?'

'Open invite on WhatsApp.'

'So you went on your own?'

'Right.'

'And you brought your wine?'

'Right.'

'Where did you get it from?'

'Not saying.'

'Your parents' wine rack?'

That got a look. And eye contact. He shook his head

again. 'From the cupboard. It's cheap stuff for Mum's sister. My auntie Joan. She doesn't like good stuff.'

'You just wanted to get into the mood, right?'

His shoulder raised. 'I don't know.'

'Gary, your father's on his way here. If you need to get a lawyer, you should tell me now and I can speak to him, and he—'

'I don't need a *lawyer*.'

'I don't think you realise how serious this is. An acquaintance of yours is dead. Three of your classmates are in the adjacent rooms here giving us chapter and verse on your relationship with Carly.'

Gary shook his head again. 'Well, Ashley doesn't know what she's talking about.'

'Okay, so you think she's grassing on you?'

'There's *nothing* to grass about. Nothing. Ashley is a *liar*.'

'Okay, but we really need to get your side of things. Then we can validate it, and get to the truth. That would be good, wouldn't it?' Vicky gave him a smile, an encouraging one. 'I mean, it could just be nothing. You could've just got spooked by the cops at the party.'

'Right.'

'I mean, we've heard that Carly's your girlfriend. But hearsay can be wrong.'

Gary was shaking his head hard now.

'Come on, it's okay. We just need the truth. That's it.'

'I didn't kill her.'

'But you saw her tonight?'

'No.'

'Okay, so when did you last see her?'

'I haven't seen her in days. Weeks, maybe. *Seriously*.'

'Was this on a date?'

'A date?' His laugh barked out and rattled around the room, jerked Vicky so much that she had to sit back. 'No, I saw her at school. That's it. Didn't even speak to her.'

'So you're not her boyfriend?'

'Whatever you've heard about me, it's all bullshit.'

'What might we have heard?'

'Whatever, it's just bullshit.'

Karen leaned forward now. 'That's what guilty people say.'

Gary looked right at her. 'What?'

'Guilty people deny. They don't speak to us. Just sit there, acting calm. You're not talking. Makes me think you killed her.'

He looked at her with anger and menace, like he could kill. 'You have no idea.'

'So enlighten us, Gary. Being honest will take a load off.'

'You should be careful who you're talking to.'

Karen sat there, arms folded, a coy grin on her lips. 'Okay.'

'I'm going to be a big shot.'

'Uh huh. And why's that?'

'I work at Indignity.'

'And what are they when they're at home?'

'You have no idea.' Gary grinned. 'They're a video games company, up on the Kingsway. I test games for them.'

'You sit and play games? That's not a job.'

'No, it is.' Gary ran his tongue over his lips. 'It's called Quality Assurance. We make sure the games don't break. It's really important work.'

'And they pay you to do it?'

'A *lot*. And I'm really good at it. I'm going to get a job there instead of going to uni. I spoke to the boss about it at the Christmas party last night. So believe me when I say I'm going places.'

'Your father know about this?'

'He's happy for me. It's a good job. One with prospects.'

Vicky saw something in him. Not just a drunk kid. Maybe the deadening of emotions was the after-effect of trauma. Or maybe he wasn't traumatised, just a dead-eyed psychopath. 'My brother plays some of these games. One where you're running around a big city, shooting people and setting cars on fire.'

Gary rolled his eyes. 'Right.'

'You know it?'

Gary smiled. 'Babe, I *test* it.'

'Shame to ruin your glorious future by murdering your girlfriend, isn't it?'

'She's—' Gary huffed out a huge sigh. 'Forget about it.'

'We can't just forget about it.' Karen leaned forward again. 'Carly's body is downstairs, going through a post-mortem. Literally means "after death". She's *dead*, Gary. Somebody murdered her. Was that you?'

The door opened and DC Considine popped his head in. 'Sarge?'

Vicky patted Karen on the arm. 'Back in a sec.' She went out into the corridor.

Considine was standing with a middle-aged man. Short, stocky, bald. Cardigan and dress trousers. 'Sarge, this is Mike Wilkie.'

Vicky fixed a hard stare at him. 'You're Gary's father?'

'I am.' Mike was twitching his fingers, rubbing them off his palms. He had the same sharp cheekbones as his son, but his face below that was a softened wobble. 'What's he alleged to have done?'

Technical terms... Hopefully he wasn't a lawyer. 'We're interviewing him in relation to a murder.'

Mike ran a hand over his head. 'A *murder*? Crapping hell. Why him?'

'Well, we gather that he's Carly Johnston's boyfriend.'

'That's complete nonsense!'

Vicky stared at him until he looked at her. 'Even so, I

need it from him. And I need it backed up by someone else.'

'Why isn't his word good enough for you?'

'Because we've got a witness on record stating that he was her boyfriend. And it wouldn't be the first time a teenager hid something from a parent.'

Mike nodded slowly. 'No, I suppose not. What's he saying?'

'That's the trouble, sir. Your son isn't speaking much. Talking about his job at a video games company.'

'Right, well. Listen, I'm not surprised.' Mike rubbed his forehead. 'Do you mind if I try and get through to him?'

'You're more than welcome.' Vicky nodded at Considine, then led Mike into the room.

Gary glanced over, then he looked away, eyes shut. Tears streamed down his sharp cheeks.

Mike sat next to his son, holding him tight. 'Hey, Gaz, it's going to be okay.'

Gary let himself be hugged. The arrogant quality assurance tester of violent video games was replaced by a lost child, looking barely even his sixteen years. 'Dad...' He buried his face in his father's chest.

Mike held him like that for a few seconds, mumbling soothing tones, but it didn't sound like words or a message. They shared the same long nose, the same cheekbones giving rise to the same sad look. 'Son, you need to tell them the truth, okay?'

Gary looked into his dad's eyes, then nodded, then rubbed away his tears. He slumped forward, elbows on the table, resting his forehead on his hands, his greasy hair dangling free. 'What do you want to know?'

'Let's start where we asked you twenty minutes ago. You and Carly.'

'There's *no* me and Carly.'

'Okay. But was there?'

'Well, maybe. Kind of.' Gary sighed. 'I don't know.'

'But you were involved?'

'Maybe. We kissed at the school disco.' Gary's lip trembled. 'I thought we were going out, but she dumped me. And I... struggled with it.'

Mike raised his hand. 'That's not him saying he's killed her.'

No, but it was the start of a motive.

'Gary, that makes me think you might have a grudge against her.'

'No.' Gary's head was shaking in tight jerks now. 'No. No, no, no.'

'Okay, let's talk about this evening. You were at the party alone.'

Mike scowled. 'You said you were going to Ian's to play Xbox with him!'

Gary shrugged. 'He was going to come along later. Had some family shit.'

Mike sat there, fuming, then thumped the table with a meaty fist. 'Gary, I can't believe you went to a *party*. I can't believe you've been *drinking*. We talked about this, Gary. You're supposed to be honest with me.'

Gary stared at his father, blinking hard. He yawned, then shook his head again. The kid was in serious denial about something. Then he burped, and lurched forward and vomited all over the table.

The rest of them shot to their feet.

Karen raced to the door and darted out into the corridor.

Mike was rubbing an arm around his son's shoulder. 'Hey, son, it's okay.'

Gary sat there swaying and looking like he was going to be sick again.

Vicky followed Karen over to the door.

Considine was outside, messing about on his phone. He looked up at the wrong time, made eye contact with Vicky.

'Stephen, can you look after the suspect for me? Take him back to the duty doctor.'

'Aye, aye.' Considine slouched into the room, then stopped dead just inside. 'Ah, Christ.' He grabbed Gary's arm, and led him out. 'Come on, son. Let's get you cleaned up.'

Mike stood staring at the table. 'I'm so sorry about this.'

'It happens, sir. Way more than you'd think.'

'You must think I'm such a bad parent.'

'I've got a wee girl myself. It's tough just now, but I know how hard it is when they're Gary's age.'

Mike nodded. 'First ten years is all about keeping them alive. Next ten is about keeping them out of jail.' He shook his head, exactly like his son would. 'Doing a great job of that.'

'Do you think he could've done this?'

'I doubt it, but then... I know it's a cliche, but they really do grow up so fast. One minute, you're putting them on swings, the next...'

'Do you know Carly?'

'I know her folks. Played squash with her father a few times, but that was years ago. We're not particularly close, mind.'

'Were Gary and Carly serious?'

'You must remember what it's like at that age better than me. Everything's so serious, like they're going to live together forever, but they'll be seeing someone else the next week. And it's hard keeping up with who they're seeing. Jane's much better at it than me.'

'Jane's your wife?'

'Right. Right.'

'And I gather that you live near the Johnstons?'

'Same street. Adelaide Place. We're at the cheaper end, though.'

'So you know Carly?'

'I do. Remember when she was yay high.' Mike held out a hand at belly button level. 'All the kids running around the street. Now she's almost a grown woman. A lot more mature than Gary.'

Vicky nodded along with him.

Mike frowned. 'I mean, girls can grow up faster, right?'

'Don't think there's a hard and fast rule, sir, but it can happen. I read something about boys' brains not being fully developed until they're twenty-five, whereas girls it's twenty-one. I think.'

'Explains a lot.'

Vicky frowned. 'By the time I was sixteen I was seeing a man in his twenties, but my brother was still going to Star Trek meetings in Dundee.'

Mike smiled at that. 'Star Trek. Well.'

'Listen, I've seen this sort of thing before. Some boys don't know what they're doing. Take things too far. Accidents happen. But we will need to continue interviewing Gary.'

'Right, I understand.' Mike shook his head. Clearly a family trait.

Karen entered the room, carrying a roll of blue paper, muttering something under her breath about Christmas Eve. She started dabbing at the sick.

'Listen, I don't know if this is any use.' Mike scratched his bald head. 'Probably isn't.'

Vicky led him away from the table to let Karen in. She wanted to get stuck in and help her, on account of Karen giving up her evening on Vicky's behalf, but Mike was dangling a juicy worm. 'Whatever it is, sir, it might help.'

'Well, it's just... I think Carly might've been seeing an older guy. Someone with his own car.'

'How do you know this?'

'I was jogging home from work one day.' Mike didn't look like a runner. 'And this car almost hit me. The driver didn't stop. And I've seen the car a few times on our street. Same plates, so I wondered if it was... Look, I saw the car dropping Carly off last Tuesday, just after I got home from work.'

Vicky hoped Forrester had the presence of mind to ask the parents that sort of thing. Hoped that the parents offered the information, and that was an active lead being investigated. 'Did her father talk about him?'

'Bill's not a talking kind of man. Football, sure. Films, telly, music. But not about who his daughter is seeing.'

Karen tossed her wad of tissue into the bin, then tore off another stretch. 'What kind of car was it?'

'A silver Skoda. You know, the kind all the taxi drivers use these days.'

'You don't think it was just a taxi?'

'Same plates every time. Seemed fishy to me.'

6

Vicky walked along the corridor, hands in pockets. 'Thanks for cleaning up in there, Kaz.'

'I'd say "don't mention it", but...'

'You want me to keep mentioning it?'

'Always.' Karen held the door open for Vicky. 'You okay?'

'Why wouldn't I be? I mean, it's Christmas Eve, we should have some wine in our bellies.'

'No, you seemed a bit weird with that kid.'

Vicky sighed. 'Just been to a few too many parties like that.'

'As a kid?'

'No. As a cop. I... I didn't go to too many parties like that.'

'You? Seriously?'

Vicky gave her that shut-up look, then walked through the door and made her way along the corridor. 'What do you make of that?'

'Well, if it *is* the same Skoda, then... Then what?'

'I don't know.' Vicky put a hand on the family room door and opened it to a crack. Hard place to be, down here in the bowels of the police station's mortuary, but no windows meant nobody could look in on you during your grief.

Catherine Johnston was still in the depths of grief. Sitting on the sofa, head buried in her hands. She looked over at the door and stood up tall, fanning a hand through her long, dark hair. 'I need a cigarette.' She reached for her bag and fished out a golden lighter and a pack warning of all the dangers. 'Do you want to join me?'

Bill Johnston was sitting next to her on the sofa, staring into space. He looked over, frowning like he hadn't quite made out exactly what she'd said, but then something seemed to click. 'Right. No, I'm fine.' He looked anything but. His face crumpled up.

Karen smiled at Catherine. 'I'll show you upstairs, madam.'

She scowled in response. 'I can manage myself.'

'There's a security system.'

'Oh. I see.' Catherine nodded, and let herself be led up

out of the room into the cold, dark night. Maybe she'd get some solace in a smoke.

Vicky sat on the armchair opposite the sofa. 'I thought you'd have been taken home.'

'I wanted to go.' Bill sat there, rubbing his hands together. 'Start breaking the news to people. But Catherine...' He sighed. 'Your boss is at the post-mortem and she wants to stay and see what... what happened to our wee girl.'

'I understand.'

Bill grimaced, squeezing his face up tight. 'The longer I stay, the worse it feels. I swear, if someone raped her, I'll...'

'I understand, sir.'

Bill glared at her, eyes narrowed. 'You got any kids?'

'Aye, she's three in March.'

Bill stared up at the ceiling, and a breath escaped. 'You never... You... Shite.' He looked back down. 'Have you got some news for us?'

Vicky sat forward, rubbing her hands together slowly. 'Not so much news as questions. I can come back if—'

'No, I want to help. Might take my mind off this.'

Vicky gave a polite smile. 'Did Carly ever mention any boyfriends?'

'Believe me, our daughter's life was a sweet little mystery.' Bill sat back, eyes closed. 'You've got it all to come. It's...' He pinched his nose. 'It's...'

'Any names spring to mind?'

'You've got one in particular, haven't you?'

'Gary.'

'Gary? Gary Wilkie? Christ no.' He frowned. 'I mean, I hadn't heard but... Well, like I say... Our daughter felt like a stranger to us at times. I mean, they played on the street when they were kids, but they grew apart. They all do.'

'Do you know if she was seeing anyone recently?'

'Like I just said, our daughter's life was a mystery. I mean, we could've locked her up, but what kind of life was that? Christ.' Bill kneaded his forehead. 'What kind of *death* is it? Letting her run wild, just to... to end up in a bloody supermarket car park.' His tears formed a droplet on the end of his nose. He wiped it away. 'Why do you ask?'

'Well, we've got a few reports of Carly getting out of a car outside your home.'

'Not that I know of.'

'A Skoda Octavia, silver.'

'Aye, that's just a taxi. Carly had a job up at the cinema. Sometimes if she was on late, they'd lay on a cab for her.'

'Sure about that?'

He nodded, but his frown betrayed any certainty. 'Why, do you think otherwise?'

'It was the same car a few times.'

'You think this car was her boyfriend?'

'We're investigating it.'

'Why?'

'Well, a car matching that description was seen entering the crime scene around the time of death.'

Bill blew air up his face. 'I wish I'd taken more of an interest in her life.'

'It's a tough line to walk, sir. A hard choice between helicopter parenting and letting them be free-range kids. It's not easy.'

'Aye, well, we've got to live with the consequences of letting her do what she bloody liked.' Bill stared at her, icy hard. 'I want to help you find who did this to her.'

'And you are, sir.'

'What aren't you telling me?'

'There's a lot I can't legally tell you, sir, under operational confidentiality.'

'Because parents can kill their kids?'

'Something like that.'

'You seriously can't think either of us did this.'

'I'm not saying you did, sir. I just can't tell you anything else.' Vicky had to look away from him. She felt her phone buzz in her pocket, but didn't feel like this was the right time to take it out and check. Then again... 'Listen, we found a phone near the crime scene. What did—'

'Samsung something or other. The deal was, if I buy it, then I get to check it whenever I want, or she buys her own.'

Which was super-invasive. And controlling. 'And did you check it?'

'It was like the bloody thing was brand new. Every single time. Wiped clean. And she kept deleting all of her messages in WhatsApp and all that. Thing was like it'd been nuked from orbit.'

Vicky got her phone out and flicked through her photos from the crime scene. There. A Samsung Galaxy A8, lying on the ground. The blingy gold model. 'What colour was it?'

'Erm, gold, I think.'

'Well, it could be hers.'

'Bloody thing. She was never off it.'

'You knew the passcode?'

'Aye. Well, Cath did.'

JENNY RAISED her eyebrows at Vicky's approach. 'Oh look, it's the ghost of Christmas present.'

Vicky sat down next to her. 'Nice to see you full of the joys of the season.'

'See if I see another Noel Edmonds jumper...' Jenny Morgan tossed the bagged-up phone onto the workbench, the cable like an umbilical cord stretching into her laptop. She snorted. 'I was looking forward to catching up on paperwork tomorrow, but no, I've got saddled with a murder.'

'Tomorrow's Christmas Day.'

'And Christmas can kiss my shiny arse.'

'You'll be on Santa's bad list.'

'It'd be a shit system if I was on the good list. And I'm on Satan's good girl's list.'

Vicky laughed. 'You're not seeing your family?'

'No.'

'Don't you—'

'*No.*'

Vicky sat there for a few seconds. As close as she felt to Jenny sometimes, at others she felt like a distant stranger. And she knew not to press her buttons. 'I'm not going to ask, okay?' She left a gap. 'How's it going with that phone.'

Jenny picked it up and, yep, it was a gold Samsung A8, slightly battered and with a spiderweb of cracks at the top left of the screen. 'Don't even know if it's the victim's.'

'You should know that you've got to eliminate it, regardless. Could be the killer's, could be a witness.'

Jenny sat back, arms folded. 'Why am I thinking that you know whose it is?'

'It's the victim's. And the code is 2868.'

Jenny smirked as she tapped it into the machine. 'Right.' She pressed a button on the screen, then set it down, and went to her laptop. 'Bingo.'

'You're in?'

'I'm in like Flynn.' Jenny typed on her laptop keyboard and the screen filled with a mirror of the phone, some app icons running top to bottom. 'Usual suspects. Whats-App, Chrome, Facebook, Instagram. Let me see...' More typing. 'And she's a careful wee lassie. Deletes all her messages.'

'Can you get them back?'

'Nope. Recovery is bad enough on emails, but it's impossible here.'

'Well, that tallies with her dad's story.'

Jenny's eyes bulged. 'He's been spying on her?'

'Mother has.'

'Lordy. Thank God I'm never going to breed.' Jenny looked around at Vicky. 'How's Bella?'

'She's good. With her granny tonight. I was supposed to have a girl's night in with Karen, but—'

'And you didn't invite me?'

'Would you have come?'

'No, I'm supposed to be sacrificing a goat up Carrot Hill with my Satanist friends.'

'I'm not even going to ask if that's a lie.'

'Ooooooh.' Jenny lurched closer to the laptop.

Vicky couldn't see what had interested her so much. 'What is it?'

'The wee minx has been using Poggr.'

'Remember she's dead, Jenny.'

'Doesn't stop her being a naughty wee rascal when she was alive.'

'Okay, so what the hell is Poggr when it's at home?'

'Don't be coy with me, Victoria Dodds. Single girl like you?'

'Jen...'

'Okay, okay. Poggr is a dating app. More like a hook-up app. Kids use it for no-strings sex these days. Log in, find a girl, find a boy, meet up for a bit of rumpy pumpy.'

'Seriously?'

'Sometimes I think you've just beamed in from Roman times.'

'You mean this Poggr is all about swiping right to like, that kind of thing?'

'See, you *do* know what I mean. You know all the—'

'I'm not into that kind of stuff, Jenny.'

'O-kay. And Poggr is about starring them, not swiping.'

'Can you see who she's starred?'

'I need to use the phone itself.' Jenny picked it up and eased it out of the bag, then touched it with her gloved fingers. Vicky hadn't even seen her put them on. 'Never, *ever* use Poggr, Vicks.'

'Wasn't planning on it.'

'Well, I've been working with the Met to shut it down. Turns out teens have been using it illicitly, reversing their ages so 15 would be 51, but it would have a photo of a young kid.'

Vicky felt a lurch in her gut. 'So paedos are on it?'

'No, hebephiles. Different age group.'

'Ever the pedant.' Vicky sighed. 'But they find young girls on it?'

'Right. And the platform are denying all knowledge.'

'Sickening.'

'Ain't it just.'

'You getting anywhere?'

Jenny nodded over to the door. 'Your boyfriend is here.'

Considine stood in the doorway, sniffing and snorting like he had a deep cold. 'Erm, Sarge?'

Vicky hauled herself up to standing, and everything ached like she was in her nineties. She walked over to the door, stooped over. 'What's up?'

'Just wondering where DI Forrester is.'

'Well, he's not down here.'

'Aye, but DS Ennis is in the incident room and he keeps pressurising me. It's inappropriate.'

Considine was someone who had inappropriate down as an art form.

'What's he asking about?'

'Well, Sarge, I've been out searching for Ennis's daughter, Teresa.'

It hit Vicky in the gut. She'd been so focused on Carly Johnson that she'd almost forgotten that another girl was missing, and the daughter of a colleague. 'Any progress?'

'A smidgen, likes. Got sidelined with bringing that daft wee laddie's old man in.' He snuffled. 'Kid sang for it yet?'

'Not yet. He's not really fit for interview.'

'Right, well, I've just spoken to Teresa's boyfriend.'

'She had a boyfriend?'

'Aye. He works at Ashworth's. Supposed to meet her after his work. Never showed.'

'You believe him?'

'We've got the internal CCTV. He was working in there. Got him swiping from the pick 'n' mix too, but aye. He wasn't there when she got taken. Or when her mate got killed.'

'He ever meet Carly?'

'Nope.' Considine held out some prints. 'Got Teresa's car driving into the Ashworth's car park, but obviously the car didn't return. Carly was definitely in the passenger seat.'

'So Teresa's definitely been taken?'

'Looks that way, aye.'

'Vicks?'

She looked over at Jenny and caught red-nailed fingers beckoning her over. 'Hold that thought.' She paced back over to Jenny's workbench. 'What's up?'

Jenny had a profile up on the screen, showing Carly's face and looking *young*. 'Well, Carly has been using Poggr since she was sweet fifteen. See her age is 21?'

'So she's one of the girls you've been looking at?'

'Not in scope, but it's a similar pattern. Trying to appear over the age of consent, anyway.'

'And have you got anything?'

'A few messages with a few daft buggers. No meetings until one of said daft sods exchanged thirty with her.'

'She hasn't deleted these?'

'Nope. Can't. And the app was hidden in a folder, presumably away from her parents' prying eyes for that very reason.'

'So who is this daft sod?

'Name of Dougie McLean.'

'Can you—'

'Already on it.' Jenny switched windows to the Police National Computer. 'By the looks of things, he's a Dundee taxi driver. Drives a silver Skoda Octavia.'

7

'Bingo.' Karen slid the pool car into the space almost before the previous occupant had left it. Close enough to get a worried look from the driver, not that he'd bothered to put his seatbelt on before driving off, instead wrapping it around him like he was a bank robbery getaway driver.

Still, he wasn't driving a Skoda. A purple Audi A4 old enough to vote.

Vicky scanned the numbers of the addresses this side of the street. 'Well done on getting a space on Lochee High Street on Christmas Eve.'

'That wasn't why I was saying "bingo".' Karen pointed over the road. 'I've got a full house. Tattoo parlour, tanning shop, Chinese takeaway and a travel agent.'

A long row of tired sixties shops, with a haberdasher

stuck in, and the sports bar at the end guarded by three mobility scooters.

'Well done.' Vicky got out into the cold air, merciful it was staying dry, then rounded the car.

Karen was at the buzzer, already pressing the button. 'Barbers and cobblers on this side. I wouldn't have got backstreet bingo with that card.'

Vicky tried to smile through the sour taste in her mouth. Not Karen's fault, but the creepy feeling that they were outside the flat of a killer. Maybe. Still, someone who'd been in contact with their victim. Regular contact.

'Jenny was saying you've been using Poggr.'

Vicky shot her a glare. 'Kaz, you know Jenny. She's an even-bigger wind-up merchant than you are.'

'Sure it's not the actual truth?'

Vicky hit the buzzer. 'I'm more of a Tinder girl.'

'No, you're not.' Karen sighed. 'Must be tough still being alone.'

Vicky sighed. 'Kaz, I'm fine. Me and Bella are fine.'

'Your mum and dad cover a lot of cracks.'

'I don't mind, seriously.'

Karen stuck her tongue and licked her lips. 'Alan hasn't been in touch, has he?'

'Why would he?'

'Just wondering.'

'Kaz, I swear, if you've—'

'No! I'm just wondering why you haven't let him know he's a father.'

Vicky shut up. The best way to stop her. Another scan of the street, but no sign of a silver Skoda. 'He's possibly not here.'

'Or he's parked—'

'Yello?' A deep voice came from the speakers, the long syllables of the bored or stoned.

'Police, sir. Looking for Douglas McLean.'

'He's no here.'

Karen rolled her eyes. 'Mind if we see that for ourselves?'

'What's it worth?'

'This is a murder inquiry, sir. My name is DC Karen Woods, with DS Vicky Dodds.'

He paused, mouth-breathing hissing out of the speaker. 'Right, you'll be wanting a discount.'

The door clicked open and Karen pushed through into the ground floor of the stairwell.

Vicky followed her in. A door was hanging open, in the dull gloom just a flickering light and a heavy citrus scent.

A big man appeared, bulky chest and massive arms. Would look menacing if he wasn't wearing acid-yellow shorts and a black Nirvana hoodie. And bare hobbit feet, thick and covered in fur. Maybe twenty-one, but already solid and one of those men with massive bulk who'd appear more muscular looking if he laid off the takeaways. Still, you wouldn't mess with him.

Not that Karen received the memo. Warrant card out, she got in his face. 'Where is Mr McLean?'

The big lump shrugged. 'Search me.'

'What did you mean by discount?'

'He's a cabbie. You lot are always trying to get free shit off people.'

Karen snarled like she was going to do just that, inside and out, just for the sheer hell of it. 'What's your name, sir?'

'Jason Matthias.' Despite the exotic name, he sounded local. Hands still stuffed in the pockets of his hoodie. 'What's he done?'

'Just need a word, sir.'

'Suppose you'll want to see his room and all that.' Jason slouched inside, his rounded shoulders heaving.

Karen let a breath go and followed him in. The smell of fresh pizza hung in the air.

Jason tried a door on the left, but didn't get far. 'Locked, eh?'

Karen checked it herself. 'Okay.'

'When did you last see Mr McLean?'

'Not today, like.' Jason slouched into a living room-kitchen, with units in the same violent yellow as his shorts, and slumped on a giant bean bag. He grabbed a video game controller off a side table and ultra-loud gunshots rattled around the room. In the harsh kitchen light, Vicky saw his hair and beard were cropped to the same length, but the moustache was slightly thinner.

Vicky stood off to the side, watching the action on the screen. A lithe woman ran around a broken cityscape, lugging a preposterous shotgun, racking it and blowing off a police officer's head in visceral detail. 'Any chance you can pause this, sir?'

'I'm playing online, so not really.' Jason glanced at the headset next to the TV remote on the sofa. An online gamer just like Vicky's brother, probably a squad of four or five big lumps pretending they were lithe women with shotguns.

What a world.

Karen was in the kitchen area, snooping around. She picked up an empty pizza box and the tubs of crust dips fell out. 'Are you and Mr McLean close?'

'Define close.' Bang bang, crash.

'Good friends.'

'I mean, we talk.'

'About girlfriends?'

'Not really.'

'Never mentioned it?'

'For Christ's *sake*!' Jason chucked the controller on the table, then pushed up to standing and stomped over to Karen, towering over her.

Vicky was halfway across the room and fumbling for

her baton when she spotted him reaching behind Karen for a slice of pizza. She stopped dead. On the screen, a Game Over screen read "You Died, GIT GUD".

Whatever that meant.

Between chews, Jason smacked his lips. 'Dougie never mentioned any girlfriends, no.'

'What about a Carly?'

'Nope.'

'So you're not really friends, then?'

'Dougie just pays me rent.'

'You own this place?'

'Oma's old place.'

'Oma?'

'Erm, my grandmother. She was German. Moved here in the sixties. My granddad worked at the Timex factory. Long story, but she died a couple years back, left it to me in her will.' Jason grabbed a tub of dip and tore off the lid, then jammed his pizza crust in a creamy sauce. 'But Dougie is absolutely radge with the ladies.'

'What do you mean by radge?'

'Well, you know. Always got at least one on the go. Number of times I got up, ready for work on a Saturday, and there's a lassie putting on her heels as she goes for a sharp exit.'

'Where do you work?'

'DC Energy.'

'Down in Carnoustie?'

'Well, aye, but our office is just round the corner from here.'

'Is it normal that you wouldn't see Mr McLean for a while?'

'Aye. Sometimes he'll get a fare to Glasgow or Aberdeen, maybe Newcastle, and be gone for like a day.' Jason sniffed out a laugh. 'I mean, Dougie's the kind of guy who'll pull the full Travis Bickle.'

Vicky spotted a *Taxi Driver* poster out in the dim hallway, the famous shot of the mohawked Robert De Niro tilting his head and his gun. She looked round at Jason, just in time to catch him staring right at her. 'I hope you mean working all night, and not getting obsessed with underage prostitutes?'

Jason smiled. 'Aye, I mean so long as he doesn't shoot anyone, right?'

'But seriously?'

'Right, no. Dougie's just a shagger. That's it.'

'So he prowls nightclubs?'

'No, he's always picking lassies up in the cab and hitting on them.'

'And sometimes he picks them up on the rank when they've been to a nightclub, aye?'

'No, Dougie's not like that. He's got the patter, eh?'

'Did he ever talk about Poggr?'

Jason looked at Vicky like she'd just had a stroke. 'Eh?'

'It's an app. Meet women and arrange hook-ups.'

'Nope.'

'But he has a smartphone?'

'One of them crappy ones.' He clicked his fingers. 'You know, the ones with the adverts.'

Vicky didn't. 'You got a number for him?'

'Aye, sure.' Jason tossed his empty tub into the sink and picked up his phone, then flipped open a black leather case. 'Here.'

Karen wrote in her notebook. 'Cheers.' She walked away, tapping at her phone and putting it to her ear.

Jason looked right at Vicky, eyes wide. 'Seriously, what's he done?'

'Can't say, sir.'

'I'm not daft. It's something connected to a Carly. And you think he's done it.'

'Right.'

Karen came back with a grim look. 'No answer.'

So Douglas McLean could've gone to ground after killing Carly.

Vicky looked at Jason. 'What car does he drive?'

'A silver Skoda.'

'He own it?'

Jason shook his head. 'All he owns are his phone and his clothes.'

'You know who does own the car?'

8

Vicky got out of the car onto the long stretch between Dundee and Broughty Ferry. The two roads were named by their target, splitting at a roundabout, with a third route heading up Strips of Craigie Road into deepest, darkest Dundee.

The taxi firm was an old cottage, extended at least twice out the back, and just on the city side, a small entrance that surely caused havoc with taxis slipping out just after the roundabout.

The circle, as the locals would call it.

And the bus route between Carnoustie, her hometown, and the city centre in Dundee. Her regular pilgrimage every Saturday, that first taste of freedom. A lot of the shops were closed now, with all of that stuff moving online. Maybe Bella would never go up there, or maybe the city centre would be all cafes and museums by then.

Aye, right.

Vicky walked across the pebbles to the office, shivering against the biting wind.

The ever-present oil rigs were sitting in the dark river. Someone had arranged lights on the nearest into a Christmas tree, a solid green wash dotted with whites and reds. No sign of the angel on top, though.

Only one car, a top-end Mercedes without the wear and tear you'd get from taking fares.

The office door flew open and a skinny man in his forties stomped out, shaking his head, holding a phone at arm's reach. 'What do you mean? Eh?'

Vicky and Karen got into formation, blocking his path.

He stopped dead and squinted at them, mouth open with a sour twist to his nose. 'Bungle, I'd better go.' He stabbed a bony finger off the screen and pocketed it, but gave them a pout. 'Cops, aye?'

'How did you know?'

He sniffed. 'Got a sense for it, you know?' He held out a hand and put on a car salesman smile. 'Alan Kettles.'

'Kettles?'

'It's an old Norse name, I'll have you know.' He was now smiling like he was chatting her up at the bar and had found his in. 'And you are?'

'DS Vicky Dodds.' She held out her warrant card. 'This is DC Karen Woods.'

'Right, and how can I help you ladies?' He was all charm now, hands rubbing together.

'Looking to speak to Dougie McLean.'

'Right.' Just like that, the pout was back. 'Come on in, then.' He strolled off back into the office.

Vicky led them inside and it was like they'd slipped through a portal to another time.

The office was done up like a posh Scottish hotel, all tasteful tartans and bare stone walls. Chunky wooden furniture.

Alan Kettles took a seat behind a massive oak desk covered in computers and phones. 'So, what's he done?'

'Just need to speak to him, sir.'

'Well, good luck with that.' Kettles sighed. 'You'd think it'd be Hogmanay, but no. Christmas Eve is our busiest night of the year. And that cheeky sod McLean isn't working.'

'He's not clocked on?'

'Nope.'

'Is that usual?'

'Happens. We're not a fancy firm like Uber or that Travis one. Old school, keeping it real. I pride myself on operating my business like my old man did. Car radios, not some daft app thing. What the hell even is an app, eh?' His pout was back. 'Trouble is, it's a bit too easy to turn off those radios.'

'Meaning?'

'Meaning that a lot of my lads run wild and pick up fares off-meter at a flat rate. "Ten quid to the Hilltown, madam, thank you. Oh, my card machine's broken, have you got cash? Well, I know a cash machine we can stop at on the way." And on my diesel and in my bloody car. Cheeky sods inflate their mileage when working legitimately, and then make up the difference when they call in "sick" and go off the bloody meter.'

'Sounds bad.'

'Och, it's the cost of doing business, isn't it? I make good coin from this. It's just the dishonesty, you know? They think I don't know. And it's not like I didn't do it when my old boy owned this place. But Dougie is the worst at it. Thinks he's getting one over on me all the time. Thinks I don't know. And lies to my face when I ask him. Cheeky sod.'

'So if we wanted a list of Mr McLean's fares for tonight...?'

'Aye, good luck. McLean's been offline, so I can't do it. And the silly bastard told me he lost his phone last night, didn't he?'

Vicky narrowed her eyes. 'He lost his phone?'

'So he said. He was in here about half-one this morning, searching for it. Think he reasoned that one of his fares had stolen it. So I couldn't get hold of him today, could I?'

'Even on his other phone?'

'You know about that, then?' Kettles smacked his lips. 'I've given you a lot of information. How about you tell me what he's done?'

'Oh crap. Was that Considine?' Karen walked over to the door, leaving Vicky and Kettles alone.

Vicky couldn't see what had spooked her, so she leaned forward to rest her hands on the table. 'Mr McLean is a person of interest in a murder case.'

'Aye?'

'Aye.'

Kettles clicked his tongue a few times. 'Let me guess, a lassie?'

'Good guess.'

'Always one for the lassies, isn't he? Knew it'd catch up with him. How'd she die?'

'Not at liberty to divulge that.'

'Shame.'

'You don't seem concerned that one of your drivers is involved.'

'Wouldn't be the first time. Don't get me wrong, I've got some good, honest lads working for me. But sometimes you take a punt and you think you're doing the right thing, but then you end up with egg all over your face and your balls.'

'Was Dougie McLean one of those punts?'

'Like trying for a hole-in-one on a par five.'

'I'll take your word for it.'

Kettles ran a hand over his jaw, dotted with stubble. 'You think he's killed this lassie and run off?'

'We don't know.'

Kettles scowled. 'He better not have. It's my bloody motor.'

'What make is it?'

'Skoda Octavia. But you know that, right?'

Vicky nodded. 'We have one at the scene of the crime.'

'Oh for crying out loud...' Kettles pouted again. 'You're going to impound it, aren't you?'

'Possibly.' Vicky got out her phone and showed him the screen grab from the CCTV footage. 'The plates have been masked.'

Kettles nodded.

'You know about this?'

'See what I was saying about them going wild? That's the main trick. They cover the plates with this spray. It's a German thing, I think, but it cleans off with soapy water. Means they think your lot can't follow them driving to Inverness on a cheeky flying cash-in-hand trip off my meter.'

'And Dougie has done this?'

'Several times, and that's just that I know of.'

'Do you have any trips to Adelaide Place?'

'Nice street. That where the lassie lived?'

'Might be.'

The door tinkled open and Karen led Considine through, looking eager as a new puppy.

Vicky focused on Kettles. 'So, are you able to go through Mr McLean's fares for, say, the last month?'

Kettles rolled his bottom lip over his teeth. 'I mean, aye, I can. But if he's been seeing this lassie for a while, maybe he's doing those trips off the books?'

The messages Jenny found went back a few months.

'Even so.' Vicky nodded at Considine. 'Can you work with my colleague here?'

'Sure.'

'Thank you.' Vicky nodded at Kettles, then walked over to Considine. 'Get a list of his fares. Look for any repeat trips, especially near Adelaide Place, then pass to the door-to-door team, get them to see if anyone knows anything.'

Considine grinned. 'Sure.'

She leaned in closer to whisper, 'And make sure he's not in touch with McLean, okay?'

'Sarge. What about you?'

'I'm heading back to base.'

9

Bell Street station was full of Christmas Eve mayhem. Two burly uniforms struggled to separate a pair of fighting drunks, middle-aged men who should've known better. Red-faced, spitting and screaming at each other.

Vicky turned the corner, glad it wasn't her problem any more. No, she needed to catch a murderer. She looked at Karen, walking lockstep with her but checking her phone. 'Everything okay at home?'

'Aye, Colin's putting the kids to bed.'

Vicky started climbing the stairs. 'Going to be a long night, isn't it?'

'We won't be able to speak to anyone tomorrow, will we?'

'Oh, I don't know. Breakfast-time buck's fizz might loosen a few tongues.'

Karen smiled at that.

Vicky stopped on the first floor. 'I'm going to see how the Grinch is doing.'

'Jenny?'

'Aye.'

'Why the Grinch?'

'Because she hates Christmas?'

Karen raised her eyebrows. 'You know that's because her boyfriend killed himself on Christmas Day, right?'

'Shit.' Vicky shut her eyes. 'How did I not know?'

'Because she didn't tell anyone?' Karen pinched her lips together. 'He jumped off the Forth Road Bridge five years ago. My Colin was First Attending Officer. We were still living in Fife. Jenny was Lothian and Borders.'

'Christ.' Vicky shut her eyes. She tried to picture it, but stopped herself. She should be tempering her words with Jenny, that's for sure. 'Can you scour the CCTV for the car?'

'What?' Karen scowled at her. 'Vicks, the plates were covered. ANPR isn't going to pick them up.'

'Aye, I know. You'll—'

'—have to manually review the CCTV.' Karen winced. '*Great.*'

'Focus on the area around Adelaide Street. See if we can pin McLean's car to dropping off Carly. Maybe picking her up. See if you can identify it at all today. Maybe he's been careless.'

'Right.' Karen set off up the stairs. 'Giving up Christmas Eve for this...'

Vicky stood there, listening to Karen's heavy footsteps trudging up, feeling the vibrations through her feet and from the handrail. She took a deep breath and tried the door into the forensics lab door. Shut, but not locked.

The place stank of rancid fish paste sandwiches and off tomatoes. Jenny was working away in the darkest corner of the room, but at a different workbench from earlier. She looked up and gave a tight nod, though she was chewing slowly. 'Evening, Vicks.' Her mouth was a mush of white, pink and red. 'What's up?'

'Just wondering how you're getting on.'

Jenny leaned back to stretch, showing her pale stomach. 'Christ.' She shivered, still yawning. But not chewing, and not reaching for another sandwich. 'Well, I've been speaking to my Met contacts just for you.'

'For the messages on Poggr?'

'Damn right. They've got what they call a "firehose". Gives them access to the whole system, including messages.' Jenny raised a finger. 'But we need to tie our request to an active investigation.'

'It's a murder.'

'I mean to our investigation.'

'And have you?'

'Don't tell anyone.'

Vicky smiled at her. 'What have you got?'

Jenny tied up her hair, then jangled the rings in her left ear, usually hidden by the walls of hair. Four of them, presumably one per year since... 'Well, I've been through Dougie McLean's message history. I'm sure you could get some cops to do this, couldn't you?'

'Very good. What has he been saying to Carly?'

'Usual. Meet up stuff. Stopped a week ago. Looks like they shifted to WhatsApp, but she's deleted all those messages, hasn't she? And I can't access them without his phone.'

'But?'

Jenny held up the bagged phone. 'Check this out.'

A woman's face filled the screen.

Hilary Jameson, 26. Younger looking, though, school age maybe.

Four miles away.

Active 26m ago.

My interests are stamp collecting and train spotting. Not looking for sex. Yeah, right. ;-)

Jenny grabbed the phone back and clicked the big green heart below Rebecca Grieve, 31. Definitely didn't look even half that age.

'Is she one of the flipped numbers age thingy girls?'

'That's how I got access to the messages. I mean, look under her eyes, Vicks. She's barely sixteen, if that.'

Vicky frowned. 'Who are these?'

'When anyone you've liked hearts your profile back, you get to message them.'

'So Dougie has been hearting a lot of people?'

'A hundred girls a day, by the looks of things.' Jenny gave Vicky a wad of papers, just like a load of text messages, and flicked through to halfway. 'Here's another one.'

Beth, 28.

I love pizza and craft beer. And big dongles.

She had a babyish quality to her.

Jenny tapped the pile of paper. 'These are their messages. Notice how quickly they get really, really dirty?'

Vicky read the first two:

I'm wet for you, big boy.

My P in your V. When?

'Unbelievable.' Vicky felt sick to the stomach. 'And this is people they've not even met?'

'Different from our day, Vicks. Don't need to buy a glass of white wine now.' Jenny turned to the next page and held it up. 'And this is the first message after they did meet.'

Vicky squinted at it:

Had fun, but let's agree no more yeh?

She gave Jenny a shrug. 'What, she's letting him down gently?'

'Problem is, Mr McLean didn't like that.' Jenny held up another sheet, the text so small there was no danger Vicky could read any of it. 'Reading between the lines, because she didn't have sex with him, he asked for the money for the meal back. And it went downhill from there.' She flicked through some pages. 'By the sixth message, he's threatening to kill her.'

Vicky sighed. 'Did she report it?'

'Don't know. What with it being Christmas Eve, the people at Poggr are playing silly buggers with my friends in the Met. They're trying to track her down and see if she's okay.'

Vicky stared at the sheets. Two hundred pages. And they were small type, too. That was a lot of girls. Would take ages going through them, to track the likely victims down.

Jesus. They all looked alike, young, but old enough to know enough. Kirsty in Aberdeen, Deanna in Perth, Alison in Edinburgh, Vicki in Dundee.

And then, right at the bottom, Carly Johnston, definitely *not* old enough to know better.

'How many of these hook-ups did he have?'

'Fifty? Sixty? Trying to figure it out is going to take a long time and a lot of your idiots. If you can spare any skulls, it'd help.' Jenny raised a finger. 'Just not Considine.'

'Damn.' Vicky tried a smile, but God, it felt hollow. She rifled through the pages again. 'So, between last February and this week, he's seen fifty-odd girls on that app?'

'That's right. I mean, the lad's got stamina.'

'Hasn't he just.'

'Have a look at this, though.' Jenny went to the last page. A set of messages with another user. Catriona, 19. 'She was supposed to be meeting up with him last night. No account activity since, though. Not even a follow-up message from either of them.'

Vicky felt that nasty twinge deep in her stomach. What if Carly tonight wasn't his first murder? 'Have you got an address for her?'

10

Vicky got out of her car and did a three-sixty. A modern primary school behind her, the playground empty for a week now. The address seemed to be the third house on their left, but the house numbering went weird around here. A row of brick boxes blessed with gardens, surrounded by a towering council block in that patch of town that wasn't Dundee, but wasn't Broughty Ferry either.

Considine got out of his car and held up his phone. 'Still no answer. Shall we?'

'I don't know. You spoke to her mother?'

'Lives in Fintry. Said they're estranged. Her word.'

'Great.' Vicky sighed. 'Any taxi drop-offs from McLean here?'

'If there were, Alan Kettles hasn't got them logged.'

'Try the house number again.'

'Okay.' Considine put the phone on speaker and the faintest ringing came from somewhere nearby.

Vicky counted to twenty. 'Okay. Let's go.' She started off across the tarmac, then up the path. The house looked empty. Curtains drawn, lights off. She waved for Considine to lead.

Considine knocked on the door and waited a beat. 'This is the police! We're looking for Catriona Gordon!'

So much for subtle.

Considine kept his eyes on Vicky, narrowing as the seconds passed by. Then another thump. 'Ms Kidd? It's the police.'

Vicky played it all through. This wasn't looking good. If McLean met her last night, Catriona Gordon was probably dead. Probably in there. 'Okay, kick it down.'

Considine was good for one thing, though. He lumbered back a few steps and took his sights. Then lurched forward with a size twelve.

The door crunched open, bouncing off the inside walls.

Considine barged into the hall and stomped across the floorboards.

Vicky followed him in, clutching her baton tight.

The place was dark and smelled of burnt toast and beans.

Vicky followed the scents into a small kitchen. Glossy

units and worktops wedged into a tiny space. A navy pot of congealed baked beans sat on the hob. An open tub of supermarket margarine lay on the counter, half turned to liquid.

On the right side of the room was a lime-green melamine table. A plate with two pieces of toast covered in beans, one slice half-eaten.

Considine swung back into the hall and locked eyes with Vicky. 'Nobody here, Sarge.'

The beans on the plate looked cold. Vicky put her hand near the pot. Freezing. The whole place had a low temperature, the kind you could feel in your bones.

A noise came from somewhere. Upstairs, maybe.

'Stephen, have you been up there?'

Considine shook his head. Typical – he'd never make a competent officer.

'Come on, then.' Vicky snapped out her baton and set off up the stairs. Keeping it slow, keeping it quiet.

Two doors, one half-open. Vicky nodded at Considine to enter the open one, looked like a bathroom.

He was in there a few seconds then came out, shaking his head.

'Okay.' Her whisper lashed around the room. Sounded way too loud. She put a gloved hand to the other handle and opened it slowly.

A small bedroom, mostly filled with a superking-sized bed, low-slung on an expensive-looking base. The blinds were open, yellow light bleeding in from the street. And ice cold, like the window was open.

No sign of anybody.

Vicky stepped over to the blinds.

Below the window. A pink leg.

Shit, shit, shit.

Vicky rested the baton on the bed and crouched down, hands out, breathing as slow as she could.

Please be alive.

A woman balled herself up on the floor, her head wedged against the underside of the table. Smudged make-up, deep-ringed eyes. Lank hair. Gripping her knees tight.

Wait. Not gripping, but tied up. With a cable.

'Stephen, get a knife or some scissors.'

'Sarge.' He bundled out of the room, then thundered down the stairs.

The woman had something in her mouth, something fabric.

Vicky reached over and eased it out. A pair of black knickers. She bagged them up, then held up a hand. 'Catriona?'

Didn't even get a look, but got a nod. She twisted her head to the side and swallowed. 'Who are you?' Local accent, barely audible.

'I'm a police officer. It's okay. You're safe.' Vicky held out her warrant card and let her inspect it. 'My name's

Vicky. I'm a sergeant. We're looking for Catriona Gordon. Is that you?'

Catriona pulled her legs tighter, shut her eyes and gritted her teeth.

Considine rushed in with a pair of orange scissors. He passed them to Vicky, blade first.

She didn't have time to correct his primary-school error, but set to Catriona's wrists. Looked like washing twine, and hard to cut through. But a few quick slices through the length of the rope to preserve the knots and she was through. Then she set about the legs.

'We believed your life was at risk, Catriona.' Vicky got through the legs a lot quicker. 'Do you want to come downstairs?'

'No.'

'It's safe.'

'He'll be back.'

'Who will?'

No answer.

'Come on, we need—'

'Douglas. Douglas McLean.'

'Is that the man you're worried about?'

Up close, Vicky could see how injured the woman was. Bruised and cut up, like she'd been punched and dragged around.

This didn't look like a consensual sex game gone wrong.

Vicky held out her hand.

Catriona stared at it for a few seconds, then gripped it tight and used it to pull herself up to her feet. She was almost as tall as Considine. Pretty, but there was a darkness in her eyes, like she wasn't in the room with them. And Christ, she looked barely ten, let alone nineteen.

Vicky offered a hand like she was with her daughter and led Catriona out of the room and into the hallway. Her breathing was getting faster with each step down. 'You're doing well, Catriona.'

She collapsed onto a chair in the tiny living room.

Vicky nodded at Considine and it took him a few seconds before he seemed to realise that he was supposed to do something. 'Call it in.' She waited for him to clear off, then gave Catriona a warm smile. 'I know how—'

'He's going to kill me.' She spread her feet wide, like she was ready to pounce at any second and get the hell out of there. 'How do I know you're not working with him?'

'We're the police, Catriona. Here is my warrant card. We were conducting an investigation and it led us here.'

Catriona scratched at her face again, chipped nails chewing at the flesh. She drew blood.

Vicky grabbed her wrists. 'Hey, it's okay. Alright? It's over. Whatever happened, whatever he did to you, it's over.' She let go.

Catriona clenched her fists, but at least wasn't hurting herself any more.

Considine came back into the room with a couple of uniforms. Sometimes the most useless could surprise you.

Still, Vicky had to shoot a glare at him in case he said or did anything inappropriate. 'You can get back to the taxi firm.'

'Sarge.' He frowned, like he was disappointed at being sidelined so soon. 'Okay. Keep me posted.'

'Will do.' Vicky focused on Catriona, cowering on her bed. 'Tell me what happened tonight.'

'I don't know if I can say it out loud with all these men around.'

'You can whisper it in my ear.' Vicky cupped her hand and put it to the side of her head.

Catriona bit her lip, her gaze shooting everywhere. She nodded and leaned forward. 'I think Doug raped me.'

'Thank you, Catriona. I know how hard that must've been. We're going to take you to hospital. They'll check you out. The officers here are going to guard this place until forensics officers arrive.'

The nearest uniform's chest deflated. Christmas Eve in a freezing house. Happy days.

Catriona opened her eyes and looked up at Vicky. 'Thank you.'

11

Alison Carmichael was a few inches shorter than Vicky and almost as wide as she was tall. Natural-looking blonde hair tied back. Staff nurse blue scrubs. 'Miss Gordon is undergoing a full examination and I will fast-track a forensic sexual assault evidence kit.'

Vicky stared back at the room off the ward where Catriona was being inspected. 'Doesn't bear thinking about, does it?'

'Sadly, it's a common occurrence.' Alison stuffed her hands into her pockets. 'I know how sensitive these cases are. Let me see how it's going, okay?'

'Thanks.' Vicky watched her go, strutting along the corridor then into the room, then collapsed against the wall. A cleaning machine was working away nearby but she couldn't see where the sound was coming from, just had that deep throb and the reek of chemicals.

And she couldn't get the thoughts of Catriona Gordon's ordeal out of her head. She had suffered one of the most brutal attacks anyone could endure. Her head would be full of self-hatred and disgust. Torturing herself, blaming herself.

Vicky had read somewhere or heard on some course about how it was the brain's way of trying to prevent it happening again. Torture yourself badly enough that you didn't get into the situation again.

The reality was so much darker than the theory. Seeing someone clawing at their skin like that. Hating their own body. When it wasn't her fault.

And whoever did it, Dougie McLean say, the sheer *callousness* of making beans on toast before he left.

Christ.

She brushed a tear out of her eye and got out her phone. A text from Considine:

Raging about McLean. Lassie was raped eh?

Expressing frustration as anger. Understanding as rage. The closest he came to caring, maybe.

Vicky called her mum, listening to the ringing. She could picture her rummaging through her handbag, scouring the contents as she searched for her phone, ringing loud enough to be heard in Edinburgh.

'Hello?' Voice super-quiet.

'Mum, it's Vicky.'

'Oh, hello, Victoria. How's it going?'

'Tough, Mum. Really tough. Listen, thanks for helping me out.'

'It's fine. The number of times your father would be called out at all hours during his days on the force.'

The plus side of having a copper father. And a mother who'd been understanding about it all. 'How's she?'

'Oh, Bella's asleep. Lasted half an hour of that film. *Frozen*, is it?'

'Aye. But that was the second time she watched it.'

'Twice back-to-back. I put her to bed and came back down to see your father watching it.'

Vicky laughed through a thick throat. 'Did he deny it?'

'Oh, of course. Still, we watched the rest of it and he's got *Die Hard* on now.'

'That's more like it. Make sure the sound's down.'

'He's got his headphones on. Cable reaches all the way to your telly.'

Vicky could just imagine him sitting there, beer in hand, cable pulled tight as he lounged back and watched John McClane killing German terrorists.

Christ, the same surname as the chief suspect, albeit differently spelled.

'Shall we put her presents out for you?'

'I'd rather do it myself, if it's all the same.'

'Any idea when you might be back?'

'You know how it is, Mum.' Vicky sighed, but felt it dragging her down into a deep well. 'But I'm not missing her Christmas for anything. Or your roast turkey tomorrow, Mum.'

'That's good to hear. Your brother's looking forward to seeing you.'

'I bet he is.'

Alison stepped out of the room, with the sort of scowl Vicky really didn't want to see.

'I better go, Mum. I'll text you when I leave.'

'You do that.'

Vicky walked over to the room, pocketing her phone as she went. The curtains were drawn, so at least she didn't see Catriona's suffering first-hand. 'How is she?'

'Well... not great.' Alison was staring into the middle distance. A big shiver and she was back. 'There's no way to prove she was raped, but she did have sexual intercourse with someone in the last day or so. Certainly since she last showered. I'd say there are signs of forced sexual activity, both vaginally and anally, presence of spermicidal lubricant, presence of micro-tears to the labia, presence of bruising to the inner thighs, forearms and neck, and of course ligature markings. The clinical findings support the victim's account you relayed to me, Vicky. Unfortunately for us, the man wore a condom.'

Superb...

Vicky had been hoping McLean had been stupid enough to leave evidence. 'But?' She hoped there was one.

'Well, we have recovered some pubic hairs.'

'How is that good?'

'Catriona is... well.' Alison coughed. She looked down at her groin. 'You know what kids are like these days. So I'm assuming it's from her attacker.'

'Not just kids...' Vicky nodded, trying to encourage the nurse. She reached into her pocket for a stack of business cards, then flipped through until she found the right one. 'Can you get in touch with Jenny Morgan about this? I want that DNA test fast-tracked.'

'Sure thing.' Alison stared at the card. 'Do you know who her attacker is?'

'I've got a good idea, yeah. Trouble is, it's related to a murder tonight.'

'The girl in the Ashworth's car park?'

'Right on the money.'

'Oh my.' Alison covered her yawn with her hand. 'Well, I'll speak to Ms Morgan right away.'

'Thanks.' Vicky tugged Alison back. 'Can I speak to the victim?'

The firmest of nods. 'By all means.'

'Cheers.' Vicky returned the kindness with a smile then slipped into the room.

Catriona was perched on the edge of the bed, staring at the TV, but it wasn't on. Wearing comfy clothes – tight leggings and a baggie jumper with an inappropriate flower pattern. And she looked even younger than in her home, just a girl. She caught Vicky's eye, then held her gaze.

Vicky stayed by the door, giving the girl some space. 'How are you feeling?'

Catriona swallowed hard. 'How do you expect me to feel?'

'There's no right way, Catriona. No wrong way, either. It's *your* reaction to a horrific incident, nobody else's.'

'Have you caught him?'

'I'll need some help with that.' Vicky reached into her pocket for her phone, but stopped short of unlocking it. 'We can do it later, if—'

'Now. Please.'

'Just a sec.' Vicky unlocked her phone and switched the phone to a voice memo app. 'I'm going to record this for evidence.' She started the app going, then found the secured email from Karen and opened it. Took a couple of steps and another password, but she was in.

Her screen filled with six faces, all men, mid-thirties. Stubble, dark hair. Some with long noses, some with open mouths.

'This is DS Vicky Dodds. I am showing Ms Gordon photo exhibit A.' Vicky held it out for Catriona, side-on to fit them all in. 'I am going to show you some photographs and if you recognise any of them, please say so and tell me from where you recognise them.' She flipped the first one.

Catriona shook her head.

Vicky flipped the page.

'Him.'

Vicky took the phone back. That was Dougie McLean, the taxi driver still at large. 'You're sure?' She held it out again.

Catriona looked at it much longer, her eyes shooting between the faces. 'Positive. Dougie. He raped me.'

'Thank you.' Vicky held the phone between them. Her stomach clenched at the thought of McLean doing this to Catriona, then murdering Carly. Escalating from rape to murder in less than twenty-four hours. 'Miss Gordon identified photo four of six, reference evidence set B.'

Catriona was frowning at Vicky. 'Will you prosecute him?'

'Once we've found him, we'll try to.'

'You mean, you haven't got him?'

Vicky didn't want to derail her, and didn't want her to even consider any blame on herself. It happened so many times. And yet it never seemed to happen to men like Douglas McLean. Their sleep was always okay. No guilt, all transferred to their victims. Still, at least Catriona was alive to help them out.

'I met him on an app. A dating one. Hook-up. Whatever it is. Thing called Poggr. You know it?'

'I've heard of it, aye. What happened?'

'That was the first time I've used that app.' Catriona rubbed at her eyes and sniffed. 'One of my friends uses it all the time. Casey. She swears by it. I did what she suggested and I liked lots of men. You know, you star them? So I liked *his* photo.' She shut her eyes, tears streaming down her cheeks. 'He had a nice smile. That was it, just that. Then I got a message back that he'd liked my photo. He was the first who liked me back. And we messaged. He seemed nice. Friendly. Flirtatious, but respectful.' She shook her head slowly, gasping for air. 'We went for a drink yesterday afternoon, then he took me out for dinner to that restaurant in the new hotel on Dock Street. You know it?'

'I know it.' Vicky had an idea which one it was, but couldn't remember the name. It was something to get Considine to look into.

'Thing is, when we were eating? I *liked* him. A lot. So I invited him back to my flat. He drove and... When we got back, I changed my mind. But he... He kept insisting on coming in for a coffee.'

'Did you let him in?'

Catriona scratched at her face again. 'I told him no. Told him to leave.'

'Did he?'

'Acted all gentlemanly about it. Hands up, you know how it is? And I thought that was it.'

'But?'

'But I got a knock on the door. Maybe fifteen minutes later. It was dark, and I didn't see who it was, just got *punched*. Again and again. Kept on doing it.' She leaned forward in the bed, hands covering her face. 'I tried screaming, but he covered my mouth with his hand. And he forced me inside my flat. I kept saying no, but he didn't listen.' Snot bubbled in her nose. 'He tried to strangle me. With his belt.' She lowered her gown to show a dark brown line biting deep into the flesh around her neck. 'Then he got the charger cable from my laptop and tied my wrists together. And then he raped me.'

The room was deadly silent.

Vicky felt her heartbeat throbbing in her neck. 'Did you see him at all?'

'It was dark.'

Shit.

Vicky stood up and cleared her throat. 'But you think it was the man you identified?'

Catriona needled fingers into her eye sockets. 'I don't know if it was.'

'And you haven't seen him again?'

'I never want to.'

'Okay, Catriona.' Vicky didn't add that she'd have to when it came to court.

Catriona was looking up at Vicky with doe eyes. 'You think it was someone else, don't you?'

'No. But we've got forensic evidence from your attacker. If it wasn't him, we will find who it was. We'll do everything we can to track him down.'

Catriona nodded. 'Thank you.'

'Okay.' Vicky ended the recording, but held her phone. 'I'm going to get back to the case now, alright? There are two officers guarding your flat, waiting for our forensics officers to attend.'

'He's going to get away with this, isn't he?'

'No, Catriona. He's not. Everything he touched in the house is being swabbed. Part of the Sexual Assault Evidence Kit, as well.'

'But he wore a...'

'Even wearing a condom, he is going to leave epithelial cells from his chest and abdomen on you, okay? They will contain his DNA. And there is other evidence. Your laptop cable, for instance, will contain fingerprints at the very least. But I won't rest until we find who did this to you.'

'Thank you.'

Vicky gave her a kind smile, then left the room. The cleaner was outside the room now, a skinny wee guy pushing the machine around, massive hi-fi headphones clamped to his skull. He was small enough he could ride on it.

She charged off down the corridor, putting her ringing phone to her ear.

Jenny answered it super-quickly. 'Vicks, I've just got off the phone to that nurse, so how the hell do you expect me to have even got the sample, let alone processed it? Besides, I'm—'

'That's not why I'm calling.'

'Oh?'

'Are you at Catriona Gordon's flat?'

'It's more a house than a flat. It's got stairs and—'

'But you're there. Good. Can you look for a laptop cable? Her attacker used it to secure her.'

'Okay.' Jenny's voice became muffled, just a shout. All Vicky could make out was the word "Jay". Then she was back. 'Vicks, just got a notification on your guy.'

'What guy?'

'McLean's phone's just been turned on.'

12

Vicky turned onto the main road leading towards the Law, hitting the accelerator hard, desperate to get there first. The car slid on the ice and she had to drag the wheel to stop it sliding up onto the verge. A long way down from up here, the lights of the city twinkling in the freezing night. Regardless, she powered on, but put her headlights on full beam to catch any more patches of black ice.

Up ahead, the monument was lit up by a high-powered torch, dancing across the stone.

Two cars sat in the small roundabout encircling it.

Vicky eased the car forward, wary of drawing Dougie McLean away, into a chase. Twenty metres away now and her headlights caught the car. A Skoda, but the light bleached it so much it was hard to tell if it was silver or not.

The other car was a battered old Vectra.

Vicky's heart fluttered – another police pool car, the one with the buggered clutch that got stuck halfway up that no amount of oil or moaning could get fully lubricated.

Her lights caught Considine standing guard by the car, except that his torch was scanning up and down the monument, reading the names of the war dead.

Vicky pulled up, blocking the way and leaving the engine running, and got out of the car, easing on a pair of blue nitrile gloves. 'Time and a place for that, Constable.'

He swung round and caught the light right in Vicky's eyes.

'Watch!' She shielded her face, but her eyesight was a big red blur. 'What are you playing at?'

'Sorry, Sarge.' Considine sniffed, then waved the torch back at the monument. 'Just reading the names. No Considines but a couple of Doddses and a Forrester.'

'And the car?'

'Right. Aye. Just guarding it for you.'

'Okay, let's see if it's him first.' Vicky stepped past him and shone her own torch into the vehicle. A surge of relief climbed out of her stomach.

McLean was in the front, behind the wheel, fully

reclined, phone resting on his chest. Looked like he was sleeping.

Vicky motioned for Considine to guard the passenger side, then waited as he gave up his reading exercise to do his actual job. A deep breath, then she grabbed her baton and opened the driver door. 'Evening, sir.'

The cabin lights came on and McLean jerked forward. His phone shot over to the windscreen and his head hit the sunroof. 'Ah, you bastard.'

'Douglas McLean?'

He looked round at her, nodding. 'Pleasure to meet you, darling.'

Vicky stood at the door post and grabbed McLean's wrist, then levered his arm out and back across her hip. The combination of the pivot and McLean's own body-weight pulled him right out onto the ground. Vicky continued the movement with the wrist, pointing it straight up, and dug her knee into the small of his back. She snapped handcuffs on his wrist.

Considine helped him up to standing.

McLean was tall, at least six foot, and with a rower's frame. Skinny waist forming a triangle with broad shoulders. A red musketeer moustache over a redder soul patch, covering a real shit-eating grin. And he was swaying like he'd tanned half a bottle of whisky. He frowned. 'Usually get a lassie's name before she pins us to the ground, doll.'

'Detective Sergeant Vicky Dodds.'

'And what have I done, Vicky?'

Vicky nodded at Considine. 'You know the drill.'

Considine cleared his throat. 'Douglas McLean, I am arresting you for the crime of rape. You do not have to say anything, but it...'

Vicky tuned out his monologue as she stepped around the car.

McLean stood there with a stupid grin on his face, like they were making a huge mistake.

Back round at the driver's side and Considine reached a gloved hand for his phone. 'I'll have that, thank you very much.'

'What?' McLean was rubbing his forehead. 'My phone?'

'Is it?' Vicky stuck it in a bag, then held it out. 'Can you confirm this is yours?'

He looked at it for a few seconds with bleary eyes. 'Think so. Christ, my head's fair nipping.'

'Why were you sleeping here, sir?'

McLean frowned. 'Search me, like.'

'That'll happen soon, don't you worry.' Vicky caught the blue lights of a squad car piling towards them.

'So. I should thank you for finding my phone.'

'Assuming you ever lost it.'

Something thumped at the back of the car.

'Anything you do say may be given in evidence. Do you understand?'

The uniforms approached them on foot now, a male and female pairing that looked like they could handle whatever Considine let McLean do to him.

Vicky stopped by the boot and listened hard. What the hell was that sound?

She ran back to the driver seat and grabbed the keys.

'Where do you think you're going with them?'

Vicky hit the open button and got a flash of lights from the car. She snapped out her baton and prodded the boot release button.

It clunked open.

A girl lay in the boot, barely able to move, fabric stuffed into her mouth. Eyes wide and staring right at Vicky, like she was pleading with her.

Vicky dropped her baton and ran her fingers over her wrists and ankles. Plastic cable ties, shit. She shouted over to the others, 'Have you got a knife?'

The male officer scuttled off towards the squad car.

Vicky eased the fabric out of the girl's mouth. 'I'm Vicky. I'm a police officer. What's your name?'

She was still conscious at least, but battered and bruised. 'Teresa. My name's Teresa Ennis. My dad's a cop.'

lison Carmichael shut the door to the room and huffed out a deep breath. 'Well, at least *she* hasn't been raped.'

Vicky nodded. Something like relief surged in her stomach. Then again, being reduced to a teenage girl *not* being raped feeling like relief? Christ. 'How is she?'

'Hard to say.' Alison stared back down the long corridor, then out of the window to the hospital's inner courtyard. 'Based on my unfortunately great experience of similar cases, I would say that Teresa's going to be okay. There's a significant difference between her and Ms Gordon. But... Miss Ennis isn't well. The abdominal injuries she sustained in the car boot... Who hogties someone in the back of a car?' Anger flashed across her lips, baring teeth. 'Who does that?'

'We have a suspect. Same man as with Catriona Gordon's rape.'

'Well, I hope you lock him up and throw the key in radioactive waste.' Alison shut her eyes, clamping them tight. 'I wish I could help, I really do, but all I've got so far is that Miss Ennis was assaulted.'

'So she's been awake all this time?'

'Sadly not. She's sustained a cranial injury, as a result of trauma to her head.'

'You wouldn't get that from being locked in a boot, though. Has someone hit her on the head?'

'I believe so. Blunt force trauma. Bottom line is she doesn't remember much about her ordeal.'

'What with?'

'Not sure. A jack, maybe? Something metallic. No lasting damage, but she's going to have a hell of a bump for a while.'

Vicky winced. A teenage girl sat behind that door, the subject of a vicious assault. Tortured, mentally and physically. Maybe torture was too strong a word. Maybe she was just restrained. The fact Teresa hadn't been raped, that didn't lessen the pain any. Or the urgency. 'Okay, so can I get a couple of minutes with her?'

Alison stared at the door, thinking it all through, then nodded. 'Okay.' She squelched off down the corridor.

Vicky stood there, trying to take enough breaths to calm her thumping heart. Not just any teenage girl, that would be hard enough, but a colleague's daughter. Someone close to her. Even if he was a dickhead.

Christ.

She pushed the door open and stepped in.

A squeal tore at her ears.

Teresa was sitting on the edge of the bed, head poking out of her top, wrapped around her neck. At least she had her bra on. 'Help.'

Vicky stepped forward. 'Are you okay?'

'I can't... I'm stuck. This.' Teresa tried to stand but couldn't. She sat there, swaying, her eyes shooting around her head. 'I feel so shit.'

Vicky eased the top back over her head. 'I think you should lie down.'

Teresa complied, as easily as a just-fed newborn, and let Vicky tuck her in to the thick bed sheet. Lying back and staring at the ceiling. 'Who you?'

Christ, she was really out of it. Whatever McLean had hit her with had really spaced her out. Concussion was a bastard.

'I'm Vicky. I'm a cop.'

Teresa's eyes shot over. 'You work with Dad?'

Vicky nodded.

'God. He's going to be *so* angry.'

'Your old man's going to be relieved you're okay. Well, as okay as can be.'

'What happened to me?'

'I was hoping you could help me with that.'

The door opened and Considine stepped in like he was entering the staff canteen at Bell Street. All swagger and smiles. 'Here you go.' He was carrying two plastic cups, oblivious to the teenager in the bed. 'Just how you like it, Sarge.'

'You daft sod.' Alison the nurse reappeared and grabbed the cups out of his hands. 'How stupid are you?'

'Just a sec.' Vicky joined Considine in the corridor and leaned in close. 'Have you gone mad?'

'Eh?'

'You can't walk into a hospital room with cups of tea!'

Considine stared at the floor like he was Bella, getting told off for naughtiness yet again. 'Trying to do the right thing.'

'Stephen, have you got hold of her father?'

'Tried. Not answering.'

Vicky took out her notebook. 'You're going to verify her story, okay? Write it all down.' She went back in and focused on Teresa, trying to assess how far the fairies had taken her.

She was scowling at Considine like he was going to assault her.

'Teresa, this is a colleague of your father's too. Stephen. He's a cop.'

She looked up at him.

Considine got out his own notebook. 'What do you remember of your ordeal?'

What part of write it all down didn't he understand?

'Nothing.'

Superb.

Didn't deter Considine. 'What was the last thing you remember?'

Teresa looked up at the ceiling. 'I can't remember anything. I remember driving. Skidding. Then, I think we saw Carly's boyfriend's car?'

Shit, she didn't know her friend was dead, did she?

Superb. Just superb.

'And what kind of car was it?'

Teresa looked over at Vicky. 'Why?'

She smiled back. 'It might be important.'

'You think *he* attacked me?'

'It's possible.'

'Is Carly okay?'

Vicky looked over at Considine, eyebrows raised so he got the message to keep quiet. 'You don't remember anything until we found you?'

'I can't think.'

'When we found you, you'd been tied up.'

'Oh man. My dad's going to kill me.'

'We're trying to get him down here. And believe me, the last person he will want to kill is you.'

Teresa's pout suggested she still didn't believe it.

'Teresa, my dad's a cop. I know what it's like.'

'Right. Do you?'

Vicky held her gaze. 'Yes. I really do.'

'Where did you see Carly's boyfriend's car?'

'Um, at the supermarket?'

'Did you see anyone there?'

'I can't think.' Teresa screwed her eyes shut. 'Wait, I remember the boot was open... they pushed me in. I... I must've been knocked out.'

Vicky stepped forward, eyes wide, trying to encourage her. 'Did you see your attacker?'

'It was dark.'

'Are you sure?'

'No. Yes. I don't know. It was really dark. Someone snapped things on my wrist and ankles. Then they... I think they hit me.' She touched her bandaged crown and checked the fingers for blood. 'They hit me and I only remember waking up in the car. Then you came to me.'

'How did you feel?'

'How do you think I felt? Sore!'

'Did you hear anything?'

'When I was taken?'

'Aye.'

'Well, I don't know. I think... Don't know.'

'Did anyone say anything?'

'Maybe I heard someone chasing Carly.'

'Did she know them?'

'Maybe.'

'When you were tied up, could you tell if there was more than one person?'

'I don't know.'

'Could you tell if they were male or female?'

'No. I don't know.'

'Okay, Teresa, it's okay to not know. Just keep telling the truth.'

'You saying I'm lying?'

'No. I'm not. Did you say something to the person?'

'I had those knickers in my mouth. Or a rag, or whatever it was.'

'Did the person or people say anything to you?'

'Not that I can think. Maybe.'

The door opened and Alison peered in.

Vicky smiled at Teresa. 'Okay. We'll be back soon, okay?' She left the room, but had to help Considine out with his cups of tea. She took hers now. 'Thanks.' She focused on Alison, sipping metallic milky gloop. 'Anything?'

'Well, the bloods are negative.'

'Negative?'

Alison nodded. 'Afraid so.'

Vicky tried to process it.

Teresa had been awake when she found her in the boot. So Dougie McLean had given her a good dunt on the head, then fallen asleep? Maybe he'd given up trying to escape, and just had tried to deflect blame.

'How do you explain the loss of memory?'

'What, aside from the dunt she took to her head?' Alison put a hand on the door. 'I'll take it from here.'

'No worries.' Vicky winced. 'Oh, and somebody needs to tell her about Carly.'

'Leave it with me. The counsellor just came on, I'll get her to have a word.' Alison smiled back. 'You've probably done enough of that tonight.'

'More than enough. A police officer should be involved, if only to gauge the reaction.'

'Well, get them to find me in the nurse's station.' Alison slipped through the door.

Vicky stepped off down the corridor, trying to get away from the room. 'Stephen, I thought I told you to stay at the taxi firm?'

'Erm, well.' He sniffed. 'Heard the call about the lad's phone come through so I hotfooted it up there. I was quicker than you. And—'

'You shouldn't have just left. Alan Kettles might be destroying records as we speak.'

'Well, there are two of your team sitting with him. Summers and Buchan.'

Christ, who put him in charge?

'I need you to get back there, okay?'

'Why?'

'Because there might be other victims. Not just Catriona and Teresa.'

'Oh, man.'

'But please stay here and gauge the reaction when Teresa's told of Carly's death.'

'Sarge?'

'Anything weird. Sure, it could be a concussion, could be post-ictal as a result of a seizure from brain ischemia, or she could be playing possum because she was complicit in her friend's murder.'

'Christ, you're a tough one.' Considine finished his tea and crumpled the cup, but there weren't any bins nearby. Vicky had no idea what happened to her cup, maybe he'd drunk both. He was going to leave it on the windowsill, but caught Vicky's glare. 'Oh. Nearly forgot. We found something.'

'At the taxi firm?'

'Aye. The daft sod had a street pick up from round the corner from Catriona Gordon's.'

'You're kidding me.'

'Nope. Just after she was raped, I'd say.'

'Why didn't you tell me?'

'I'm telling you now.'

'This is important!'

'Calm the beans, Sarge. I sent that clown Buchan round to get a statement.'

'You've got their *name*?'

'Aye, spoke to the wifie on the phone. Joan Inglis. Lives up in the Hilltown, seeing her brother. Boy's just lost his wife, so they were having a wee tipple.'

'But if she was too far gone when—'

'She's teetotal, Sarge. Brother's a lush, but she was completely compost mental.'

'It's compos mentis.'

'What is?'

'Never mind, Stephen. Thanks.'

'Don't mention it, Sarge. Except to DI Forrester come annual appraisal time.'

'Can you get a statement from her?'

14

W here the hell was he?

Vicky felt like she'd been standing outside the interview room for hours, but it had been less than ten minutes. She checked her phone again, but nothing. Still, maybe anything shy of an hour was over-optimistic for a duty doctor on Christmas Eve.

'Sergeant?'

She swung around and saw a short uniformed officer plodding along the corridor accompanying a much taller man, swinging his briefcase in his hand. Black suit, white shirt, sky-blue tie. He looked like he meant business, his face flabby around an aggressive snarl on his tiny features. He stopped and thrust out a hand. 'Bruce Watson of Nelson-Caird & Watson. Here to represent Mr McLean.'

Vicky nodded at the uniform. 'Thanks.' Then scanned Watson's face. 'How long do you need with your client?'

'I got enough information over the phone.' Watson checked his watch. 'Be wishing you a Merry Christmas in just over an hour. Let's just get him back home, aye? Nice family Christmas tomorrow.'

'I've visited his home. He hasn't got any family.'

'Except for his poor mother, all alone now.' Watson's snarl turned into the most pathetic small child pout. 'Father left her last summer and she was looking forward to a Christmas with her only son.'

Vicky knew precisely what game Watson was playing at here but still felt that tickle in the back of her throat. The sympathy card, but he was playing it way too early. 'Your client should've thought about his poor mother before he raped one girl, murdered another and kidnapped a third, shouldn't he?'

'That's a moot point.'

'A *moot point*?' Vicky felt her eyebrows jerk up. 'Excuse me?'

Watson put his hand on the door. 'I assume you're intent on seeing this charade through?'

'Oh yes, very much.'

'Well, in that case...' Watson entered the room and thwacked his briefcase down next to McLean. 'Evening, Douglas.' He thrust out his paw. 'Bruce Watson. Let's try and get you out of here, aye?' He sat opposite Karen, but she didn't look up at him, stayed scribbling in her notebook.

Vicky held the door open with her foot, so she could keep her eye on Watson. Not a lawyer she'd encountered before and, while Dundee wasn't exactly engulfed with the same crimes as Edinburgh or Glasgow, they still had their fair share of Machiavellian criminal defence lawyers. She opened the door wider and stepped into the room.

Just as her phone rang.

She fished it out and checked the display. *Considine calling...* Vicky sighed. 'Better take this.' She nodded at Karen to get the recording going, then stepped back out.

Watson smiled at her. 'You've got to try harder than that.'

'Two seconds.' Vicky let the door shut and answered it. 'What's up?'

'Just at that woman's address now, Sarge.'

'Which woman?'

'Eh, the Inglis woman. You know, Catriona Gordon's neighbour's sister? I've got her statement and it checks out with another of Catriona's neighbours. One of those curtain twitchers, but she photographs the cars.'

'Blessed be the curtain twitcher.'

'Still, it backs up her story. McLean left the flat at just after eleven and took Mrs Inglis up to the Hilltown. Assuming he was the one who raped her, that's cold, eh?'

'Very cold.'

'I thought you were staying at the hospital?'

'Aye, I did. Lassie boked all over that wee nurse's shoes. Not a pretty sight.'

'Think she was genuinely upset?'

'Just called and checked. Aye, still crying. Going to sedate her soon. Poor kid.'

Vicky felt her eyebrows lift. Sometimes the odd ones surprised you.

'Oh, and Sarge, I've just been around to that restaurant?'

'The hotel one?'

'Aye, it's called the Chez Mal Brasserie.' Considine said it with a fairly authentic French accent, all rolling Rs. 'In there eight till nine.'

'On the dot?'

'Pretty much, aye.'

'Okay, thank you.' Vicky killed the call and tried the front desk downstairs. 'Marko, do you know where the duty doctor has—'

'Aye, aye, aye. He's busy. Six-man brawl on Reform Street. The two arseholes not in hospital look like a Tarantino film, so he's a bit busy.'

'It's just a quick one. Can you ask him if Dougie—'

'Aye, he's okayed him for interview.'

'Not that. Ask him to call me.'

'Sure, sure. Here! You can't do that in here! Oh for—' And he was gone.

Vicky put her phone away, sighed, then entered the interview room. 'Thanks for attending so swiftly, Mr Watson.' She took her seat and got a nod from Karen – everything was up and running. 'I appreciate it's Christmas Eve, so I'm hoping you will just give us a full confession and we can all go back home to our families.' She paused. 'I mean, except you, Mr McLean.'

He ran a hand down his face. 'I'm innocent.'

'Sure about that?'

'You're restraining my client on some trumped-up charges, which are frankly ridiculous.'

'Mr McLean, do you know a Catriona Gordon?'

He frowned. 'You mean Catriona?'

'So you do know her?'

'Well, aye. I mean, I met her on an app.'

'Which one?'

'Can't mind.'

'That because you're doing the same trick on so many services?'

'What trick's that, sugar?'

The brass neck on him... 'We're talking about Poggr.'

'Right, aye.'

'You meet a lot of girls on there?'

'It's not as good as others, but aye. Sure. I'm popular.'

'Did you meet her in person?'

'Met her for a drink. I mean, I was driving, so I just had a Coke.'

'And then?'

'Went for a nice meal. Chicken and chorizo thing at that place down on Dock Street. She had some pasta thing, I think.'

'And then?'

'I dropped her at home. She wasn't giving me any signs, likes.'

'What does that mean?'

'You know, asking me in for a coffee. Leaning over for a kiss. None of that.'

'So, you just dropped her off?'

'Sure did.'

'Quite the gentleman.'

'Hey, being gentle is one of my best traits.'

'Sure it is.'

'What time was this?'

'I'd need to check, wouldn't I?'

'When did you meet for that drink.'

'Half six.'

'Early.'

'Both busy people.'

'And then dinner?'

'Erm, about an hour and a half later.'

'So eight?'

'Sounds right.'

'When did you leave to take her home?'

'Weren't in there long. She seemed to be up for it, so

suggested going.'

'Okay, so nine?'

'If you say so.'

'I do. We've got evidence of it.'

'So why are you asking me?'

'It's all part of the process.'

'Sure it is.'

'The next movement we've got for you is collecting a fare opposite Miss Gordon's flat.'

'That so?'

'Half past eleven.'

'So? I was working.'

'Just so happened to come back there?'

'Nature of the beast, isn't it? End up back where you started sometimes.'

'You turn the meter and radio off then?'

He brushed a hand on his neck. 'Must've done, aye.'

'Then you turned the radio back on and just so happened to be there.'

'If you say so.'

'See, that's one way of looking at events. Another is that you left Miss Gordon's home, waited, maybe even drove around the block, then walked back, rang her doorbell, punched her, raped her, tied her up and left her. Then you returned to your car and took the fare.'

McLean pinched his nose. 'That right, aye?'

'But not only that, while Miss Gordon was tied up in

her bedroom, you made yourself beans on toast. But you didn't finish it. Why?'

'Not saying anything.'

'Your chicken and chorizo dish not too filling after all?'

'No comment.'

'So, that's it? That's all you're giving us?'

McLean sat back, folding his skinny arms over his chest. 'Would need to check with the boss what I did next.'

'You left the cable behind.'

McLean's eyes bulged. 'Cable?'

'The laptop power cable you choked her with. A Dell, I believe. It's being run for prints. And the washing twine you bound her with, but that'll be harder to trace.'

He was blushing now. Looking at his lawyer, eyes darting everywhere. 'It was something she asked me to do.'

'What was?'

'Break into her house, tie her up and rape her.'

'No, it wasn't.'

'Tell you, it was. Some lassies are really into kinky shit and straight off the bat. We were talking about it in the restaurant, about how she had fantasies about a filthy cabbie. So I enacted them.'

Vicky just knew this would happen. The lying, the victim blaming. 'Mr McLean, the good news is that, now you've been arrested, your prints are on the system, along with your DNA. We can match you with the assault on her. You'll be off the streets for years.'

'This is complete bollocks.'

'Is it? Because from what I can see, we've got you. Just admit it. Please. Let us get home.'

'I haven't done a thing to any lassies. Just gone about my business like an honest man.'

'Like one. But not one.'

'I haven't done anything.'

'Okay, let's talk about the young girl tied up in the trunk of your car.'

'What?'

'Come on, you saw her. Did she have a fantasy about a filthy cabbie too, aye?'

'You planted her.'

'We planted a teenager in your boot? Right. Did we clonk her on the head too?'

McLean let out a sigh. He had nothing.

'Okay, so how about you tell us about Carly Johnston?'

'No idea who you're talking about.'

'Really? Because you've been chatting to her on Poggr.'

'Oh, Carly? Wait.'

'You know her?'

'Aye. Dated for a bit.'

'Were you intimate?'

'Obviously.'

'Why did you kill her?'

McLean frowned. 'She's *dead*?'

'Very good. You know she is.'

'Seriously?'

'Come on, son. Your car was seen leaving the scene in a hurry. Did she not have fantasies about a dirty cabbie, is that why you killed her?'

'This is bullshit.'

Vicky stared at Watson. 'These theatrics aren't helping his case any.'

Watson leaned over to whisper in McLean's ear for a good few seconds, then McLean nodded. He sat forward, scratching at his neck. 'Look, the truth of it is that I've been seeing Carly for a few months. On and off, but mostly off. It's just a sex thing.'

'She see it that way?'

He shrugged a shoulder.

'You weren't going to meet her tonight, were you?'

'No.'

'Why are you lying?'

'I'm not. I haven't heard from her in days. A week, I think. I ended things.'

'Sure.'

'Seriously. She *loved* us, even told us. And Christ, I hate that word. She was getting way too clingy for my liking.'

'Too clingy?'

'Aye, I'm not ready to settle down and she definitely

isn't. I like her, but seriously. I don't want to settle down.'

'Settling is not going to be a concern for you for a good few years, Mr McLean.'

He sniffed.

'So you're saying you haven't seen her in days?'

'Not since, what, Tuesday, I think. Took her for a drive up the Law, and broke it off. She walked off home. Not far from there. Wouldn't even give us a farewell blow job.'

'She's *dead*.'

'Aye.'

Vicky shut her eyes. Yet another empty psychopath. How did these people sleep at night? Did they? Did it ever catch up with them? 'Why did you have a seventeen-year-old girl in the boot of your car?'

Another shrug. 'Search me.'

'Are you saying you won't even attempt to explain abducting her?'

'I'm saying I can't explain it.'

'Try. Give it your best shot, Dougie.'

'Piss off. Look, youse can believe what you want. I'm innocent.'

'The same girl's car was at the location *you* arranged to meet Carly at.'

'I did nothing.'

'We'll be able to prove it. Our forensics team will get location information from your phone.'

'Sure they will. And that location won't be mine. I lost my phone, then someone knocked me out.'

'Come on, you don't expect me to believe you, do you?'

'I don't really care what you think, love. I lost my smartphone, then woke up with it on my chest. You woke us up and I catapulted it on the dashboard.'

'Right. That old chestnut.'

'Damn right. Feel a bit stupid about it, if I'm being honest.'

'I wouldn't know, I keep waiting for you to be honest.'

'Aye, I didn't have a passcode on it. Lucky someone didn't clear out my bank account. Sounds like someone's been using my Poggr account, though, trying to get in touch with Carly.'

Vicky wanted to get him to play it out, let him make as many mistakes as he could, then snare him in a trap. 'Okay, so what have you been doing?'

'I've been working.'

'All day?'

'Since ten.' He sniffed. 'Absolute ball-ache as I won't get my new phone until after Christmas now and the boss is a bit of a dick about things like that. I mean, the car's his but the phone's mine.'

'Okay, so you've been working. How did you come to be asleep at the Law monument with a teenager in your boot?'

'When I realised it was gone, I kept calling my own

number, right. Thing cost us a fortune and they could be calling Australia on it. Eventually, the boy answered and said he'd found it. I turned up to meet him, strangely enough up at the Law, but when I turned up, someone grabbed us from behind and...'

'And what?'

'Well, I mean...' McLean scratched his chin. 'I tried to fight him off, but he was choking me.' He leaned forward and wrapped his arms around his throat. 'Grabbed us, like in WWE, eh?'

'You think that proves any of this?'

'What, you think I could've done that to myself? Nae danger. Your doctor said I was lucky not to suffer brain injury from it.'

'Even if it meant getting off with rape, murder and abduction?'

'I'm telling you, this boy attacked me. Knocked us clean out.'

'Right.'

'I swear this is the truth. When you woke us up, I swear I was seeing two of you. The worst kind of three-some, I tell you. Two cops trying to arrest you.'

Vicky let it bounce off her, kept her expression neutral.

'Like I said, it was one of my fares from last night who nicked my moby.'

'Which fare was it?'

'He didn't say.'

'And you can't remember?'

'I mean, no. I can't.'

'You recognise him?'

'Well, I've seen him a few times but can't place him.'

15

Vicky popped her head into the Incident Room and gave it a quick scan. The whiteboard was cleaned and the dull tang of the pens attacked her nostrils. Rows and rows of computers, with only two officers hammering away at the keyboards.

And she got caught.

'Vicks.' Ennis jogged over, hands in his pockets.

'Careful you don't trip.' Vicky was smiling.

'Eh?'

'Running with your hands in your pockets, Ryan. Schoolboy error.'

He frowned. 'Right.'

'Why are you still there?'

'Trying to be useful, Vicks. Setting up this room for the gaffer. Thought this case might go on for a while.'

'Wouldn't be so sure.' Vicky patted his shoulder. 'I meant, why aren't you with your kid?'

'Eh?'

'Teresa's safe.'

'What? Why didn't anyone tell me?'

'Considine called you.'

'That laddie... I swear...' Ennis walked back into the room and grabbed his knee-length coat. 'Where was she?'

'She was in the boot of—'

'What?' Ennis stopped in the doorway. 'In the *boot*?'

'Ryan, just go and—'

'Whose boot?'

'Ryan, seriously, you—'

'That cabbie? Right? Where is he? Downstairs?'

'No, he's—'

'I'm going to kick the absolute living shite out of him.'

Vicky grabbed Ennis by the arm, digging her thumb into his wrist like her old man taught her, and pushed him into the doorway. 'Don't be so bloody stupid. We need the conviction to stick, not for you to go all medieval on him.'

'What are you still doing here, Ry?' Forrester was strolling along the corridor, arms out like he was marching. He stopped and frowned at them. 'What's going on?'

'Nothing, sir.' Vicky let him go. 'Ryan was just heading to Ninewells to see Teresa.'

'Thought you'd already be there, Ry.' Forrester shook

his head. 'Go on, spend time with Teresa and Dawn. It's Christmas Eve, after all.'

Ennis looked around at her, scowling, but a few seconds later he gave up and nodded. 'Fine.' He folded his coat over his arm and walked off, tapping something into his phone.

'Some boy.' Forrester watched him go, shaking his head again. 'Any idea how I can get rid of him?'

'Promote him.'

Forrester barked out a laugh. 'Some arsehole promoted him already and it's too high a level for him.' He sighed. 'Anyway, good work on finding his girl.'

'She's in a really bad way.'

'Young enough to get better, though. Not like anything truly bad happened.'

'Bad enough, sir.'

'I suppose.' Forrester pinched his nose, then led her into the Incident Room. 'Ah, just what I like to see. A sense of order in the world.' He sat down at a computer but didn't log in. 'Reason I'm talking such shite is I'm just back from the PM. Brutal seeing a young lassie laid out like that. Only upside is that Carly wasn't raped.'

Vicky collapsed into a chair. '*Wasn't?*'

'Nope.'

'So why did Arbuthnott say—'

'She didn't. Said it was a possibility. We maybe coerced her into saying it.'

'Sounds like you're defending her.'

'Well, she's given up her Christmas Eve to carve up a lassie's body like a turkey, so I kind of owe her one.'

'Did she give you anything?'

'Not really. Strangled. Some bruising on the neck, petechial haemorrhages in the eyes. You know the drill. Pretty much the same MO this McLean lad used on Ryan's kid and on young Carly.'

'Lot of tying up going on. Catriona Gordon was tied up too... And Catriona was definitely done by Dougie.' Vicky frowned. 'But Carly wasn't tied up, just strangled?'

'What are you saying?'

'I don't know. Have you got the photos?'

'Of her?'

'Of the knots.' Vicky got out her phone and found the bindings Dougie McLean had used on Catriona, where she'd been ultra-careful at releasing. She held it up. 'Dougie's had proper knots, see? Lots of them all symmetrical and obsessively neat.'

'You know a thing or two about bondage?'

'Sir, I'm going to pretend that's an inquiry as to my professional history.'

Forrester was blushing. 'Aye, course it is.'

'Well, on Teresa...' Vicky found the photos. 'See? Amateur as hell. Nothing like on Catriona.'

'Right.'

'That's it?

'Come on, Doddsy, it's—'

'Sir, we should be getting a warrant. Go to his flat again, get into his room. Might find similar knots and books on bondage, fetish porn. But it doesn't explain why Teresa's knots look like I've done it. And I didn't get a badge for knots in the Brownies.'

Forrester patted her on the arm. 'Cheer up. We've got him.' He got up and stretched out. 'And let's get home, raise a glass with our families and celebrate a good collar. They've put up with enough.'

Vicky sat there, arms folded, something rattling around in her brain.

'I know that look. Your old man's got one exactly the same. What's up?'

She looked up and met his narrow-eyed stare. 'I'm just not so sure, sir. The stuff about his phone going missing. Plus the fact he didn't rape Carly before she died. It all feels a bit too convenient. Or just... I don't know.'

'Doddsy.' Forrester huffed out a sigh. 'McLean raped Catriona Gordon. He abducted Ry's lassie. He killed Carly. Sometimes murder doesn't always have to follow rape. Sometimes they lose the ability. Not everyone associates violence with arousal.'

'Or he didn't do it.'

Forrester held up his thumb. 'Catriona, eyewitness, raped.' His forefinger. 'Teresa, found in the boot of his car, abducted.' Then the middle finger, but not pointing at

Vicky. 'Carly, murdered where she was going to meet him and where Teresa was abducted from.'

Vicky couldn't look at him for much longer.

'Look, I'm going home, Raven's orders. You can bugger off and watch *Die Hard* with your old man. Whatever.'

Vicky slowly got up. 'I think we need to check it all through, sir.'

'It's Christmas bloody Eve. You're here as a favour to me, that's it. Why don't you bugger off and spend some time with your kid?'

Vicky nodded. But the taxi firm was on the way home.

VICKY HIT a wall of traffic on the Broughty Ferry Road, that short gap between the town and the city, both long since merged. Blue lights flashing up ahead probably meant some daft kid went hammering along here at sixty and caught the ice, then another car. She'd seen it a few times over the years.

That same CD was stuck in the player, but at least it played. Seemed weird listening to the *Frozen* soundtrack without Bella in the back singing along, but Vicky knew all the words too, and having it play softly in the car was better company than Karen, asleep in the passenger seat.

Not even midnight. Last of the party animals.

Vicky got through in a wave of cars, all taking it slow

on the black ice. A poor uniform was shaking grit over a stretch, blocked off by a squad car. And sure enough, a souped-up Peugeot was wrapped around a lamppost. The driver was sitting on the wall, rubbing his head but laughing, so at least he hadn't ruined anybody else's Christmas.

Vicky's phone rang. *Dad calling...*

She got that jolt of fear. Never a good thing when he was ringing her. Made her think of all the shit that could happen to her mother.

She hit the button on the wheel to answer it. 'Hey, Dad, you okay?'

'Aye, totally fine.'

'So why are you calling me?'

'Well, just noticed a few missed calls from you to her. Your mother's asleep, sitting on your chair. That chainsaw sound you can hear is her snoring.'

'Ah.' Vicky felt herself smiling. 'How's *Die Hard*?'

'It's always cracking, my girl. Just about to put on the third one, as it happens.' Dad yawned down the line. 'Everything okay?'

'Just heading home now.' Vicky eased towards the roundabout. Straight ahead was Carnoustie and home, about twenty minutes away, fifteen if she could get the run of the lights around Monifieth.

Warm house, cold wine.

And just up ahead to the right was the taxi firm. Where Considine was going through Dougie McLean's taxi trips, looking for evidence to back up a really solid conviction, at least in Forrester's eyes. She should really let him go. Probably still lived with his mother, and she'd be wondering where he was. She would've let him go if the stupid sod had answered his phone.

'Dad, how many times did you catch a murderer at Christmas?'

'Way too many. Numpties in the pub, open and shut cases. But there was that serial killer case, too.' He paused for a few seconds. 'But mostly it was just dafties knocking lumps out of each other, taking it too far.'

'And did you get pressure to head home and have a family Christmas?'

'Seems like Christmas is the only time when senior officers insist you bugger off home.'

'Right.' Vicky indicated, just short of the roundabout, and pulled off the road. 'I'll be about half an hour, Dad.'

'Sure thing. But I've got a couple of hours of John McClane here if you need it. And a fair few tins of beer.'

'Don't tempt me. Love you, Dad.'

'Love you too.'

Vicky hit the call end button as she pulled into the last free parking space, next to Considine's car – at least he was here.

Karen was looking at her, yawning and frowning. 'What's up?'

'Just going to relieve Considine.'

'Okay-doke.' Karen sat back, eyes closed.

Vicky left *Frozen* playing and got out into the bitter night. The wind had picked up from earlier, tossing an icy blast towards the city. She battled through it as she made her way over to the entrance. The door took a bit of effort to open.

Considine and Alan Kettles were sitting at a computer, laughing and joking like a pair of kids at school dicking about on the internet.

Considine glanced over at the door and shot to his feet like he'd been gossiping about Vicky. 'Sarge? What are you doing here?'

'Just letting you know you can get off home, Constable. Have a good Christmas.'

'Just me and the Xbox, eh?'

'Not going to a family Christmas?'

'Mum's in Spain with her new boyfriend. God knows where the old man is.'

Vicky felt that pang of guilt, that she should invite him to her family Christmas. But then, it was Considine and he'd probably engineered it so he could spend all day playing Xbox. 'Sorry to hear that.'

'It's fine, Sarge. Anyway, we're not far off finishing here.'

'Oh?'

Considine gave a brief glower, like he didn't want her

inspecting his work, but he put on a smile quickly enough. 'Just been going through McLean's fares.'

'And?'

'Well, Mr Kettles has been putting his back into it, have to say.' Considine smiled at the owner. 'After all that, we've got some big gaps to fill tomorrow.'

'Tomorrow's Christmas.'

'So it is. Well, on Boxing Day then.'

'You're off until the 27th, Stephen.' But something sat uneasy with her. 'These gaps, could he have been raping and killing?'

'Exactly, Sarge. Exactly. What you were saying about the lad's phone, about some boy calling him.'

'I didn't tell you that.'

'No, that's right. Kaz texted us. Couldn't back it up. But *he* can.' Considine grinned at Kettles like God knows what. Like he was trying to impress the alpha male in the herd? Maybe. 'Now we've recovered the car, it'd be useful to get hold of it.'

'Stephen, it's evidence.'

'Aye, but—'

'There was a kidnapped teenage girl in the boot.'

'Aye, Sarge. If you'd let me finish?'

Vicky raised her eyebrows. 'On you go.'

'Way he explains it, McLean was reporting no fares and was off radio, which is our gap.'

'But?'

Considine frowned. Then looked over at Kettles. 'How about you explain it?'

Kettles sat there with the composure of an expert being asked to provide his opinion in a case, like that mansplaining statistician last year. 'Like he says, my boys have been going off radio and running wild for a few years now. Big issue for me, as it's my car and my diesel. But.' He raised a finger. 'I let that play to my advantage.'

Vicky wished he'd cut to the chase like in one of her dad's films. 'How?'

'Been in this business too long to let my drivers run wild for long. The lads and lassies have to return the motors to me for MOTs and services. Simple task to replace the radios for all the cars over a couple of months, and to put a GPS tracker in the radio that runs even if the power button is turned off.'

That could shut the door on the case, and get her home. 'How easy is it?'

'Piece of pi— *cake*, love.'

'But?'

Kettles grinned at Considine. 'See what you mean about her.'

Vicky knew she could dive headlong down that rabbit hole, but needed to stay focused here. 'How do you—?'

'You're a smart cookie, you.' Kettles shook his head, grinning away. 'I need to get at the motor itself, plug the laptop in and it'll let me download the data from the GPS tracker. Then I can tell you exactly where it's been for the last seventy-two hours.'

'Why that long?'

'How long it takes until the memory chip fills up, eh? I can usually concoct an excuse to get it within that window, then I can nail their balls to the wall if they've been too cheeky. I'm a reasonable man, I did it myself when I was—'

'So if we take you to the car, you can do it?'

'Less than a minute, love.' Kettles grabbed his laptop. 'Just show us where it is and I'll see if Dougie's story checks out.'

16

Vicky pressed the doorbell again, shivering in the cold, the night seeming that bit darker. 'Come on, come on, come on.'

Karen stood there, yawning into her fist, bleary eyes scanning the house. 'They're in.'

'Aye, but not answering the bloody door.' Vicky checked her watch. Two eighteen. Christ, how did it get to that time? She pressed the button again.

Along Adelaide Place, the other house they'd visited – Carly Johnston's parents. Lights on inside, but low. The sign of grief.

The door opened and a woman peered out. Eyes lined with stress and fatigue. Dressed in leggings and a top, but like she was going for a run, instead of bed. 'Can I help?'

No complaint about it being the middle of the night.

'Mrs Wilkie?'

'That's right. Jane.' She didn't hold out a hand. 'And you are?'

'DS Vicky Dodds.' She flashed her warrant card. 'This is DC Karen Woods. We're here to speak to your son.'

'What's he done?'

That hit Vicky with a frown. 'He was arrested earlier this evening. Your husband was—'

Jane shot off into the house. 'GARY!'

Vicky glanced at Karen, then followed Jane inside.

The place was beige. Everywhere. Everything. A beige rug over pale floorboards in the hall. Beige pictures on the beige painted walls. Beige carpet in the living room, with beige wallpaper.

Mike Wilkie sat in the living room on a beige leather couch, in front of American wrestling, big muscular guys with long hair throwing each other around. He looked over at them, gave a nod, then went back to his wrestling, sipping whisky from a glass.

'YOU SHOULD'VE TOLD ME!'

Vicky followed the din through the house to a large kitchen, a room that had taken all of the colour from the house and put it on display. Bright-red units, a baby-blue Aga, mid-orange carpet and deep-purple dining table with matching deep-purple chairs.

Gary Wilkie was standing by the stainless-steel American fridge, the only thing in the room that had no colour.

He was clutching a bowl, spooning cereal into his mouth. Milk dribbled down his chin. Probably the first food he'd managed since decorating his shoes in the interview room. 'Didn't Dad tell you?'

Jane stood way too close to him, fists on hips, looking like she was going to punch a Wilkie, but hadn't decided which one. 'So you were arrested?'

'Aye.' Gary looked over at Vicky, then hid behind his cereal bowl. 'They did it. Those two arrested me, Mum.'

Jane focused her anger on Vicky. 'What happened?'

'We had reason to believe that your son was involved in the murder of Carly Johnston.'

'Carly?' Jane dipped her head. 'She's dead?'

'I'm afraid so.'

'I used to babysit for her when she was wee. Sorry, I didn't know. I was out at a friend's for a catch-up. Why did you think Gary did it?'

'We *thought* he'd killed her because he ran away from us at a party. And couldn't explain his movements.'

'But?'

'His assistance, and that of your husband, led us to another suspect, Carly's boyfriend.'

'That taxi driver?'

'Correct. You've seen him?'

She sighed and her fists slipped from her hips. 'Aye, I've seen him. The taxi driver, aye?'

'The reason we're here, Mrs Wilkie, is that we believe

that her boyfriend's last fare before he lost his mobile phone was to this address.'

Gary tossed his bowl in the sink with a clatter. Milk sprayed up, cereal lumps sticking to the splashback tiles and sliding down. 'Why does everyone think it was me?'

Vicky approached him, slowly and carefully, mindful of his tendency to run. And to vomit. 'When we spoke to you earlier, you told us you were at a work night out last night. The video game company?'

Jane got between them, mama bear protecting her cub. 'That's true. He was out.' She wagged a finger at Vicky. 'But he's too young to drink.'

Aye, right. Vicky focused on the mother. 'Did Gary get a taxi home after it?'

Gary shook his head.

'Mrs Wilkie, did you pick him up?'

Jane shook her head now. 'I didn't, no.'

'And your husband?'

'He was out himself.'

Nailed. Vicky focused on Gary. 'When you took the taxi last night, did you steal his phone?'

'Whose phone?'

'Carly's boyfriend.'

'No!'

'You sure about that?'

But Gary wouldn't answer.

'Here's what we know happened. You caught a cab home with—'

'I didn't!'

'You did. We know you did. A pick-up in the city centre, driven here. You told us you were at the Indignity party, which we know was at the Malmaison in the centre.'

Gary looked defeated now, his head slumped on his chest.

'You stole his phone, arranged to meet Carly, then you stole a car, kidnapped Teresa.' Vicky held his gaze. 'Why did you do it?'

'I didn't do anything.'

'Son, right now, you really need an alibi for this evening.'

'I didn't kill Carly!'

'Oh, so who did? One of Santa's elves?'

'How dare you talk to my son like that!'

'Mrs Wilkie, we know your son was in a relationship with Miss Johnston for—'

'Bullshit!' Gary lurched forward and launched his fist at Vicky's head.

She caught it and twisted his arm around his back, then forced him over the kitchen table.

'This is bullshit!' Gary was shooting his head either side to get at Vicky, but she had him pinned down good and proper. 'Carly is a witch!'

'A witch, right.'

'You don't know what I've been through!' Gary went limp, collapsing against the counter, his body rocking with tears. 'What she put me through...'

Vicky snapped out the handcuffs and rolled them around his wrists. He stayed there, sobbing against the worktop. 'What did she put you through, Gary?'

'Hell.' He turned around, glaring at her. 'Carly and Teri, they made my life hell!'

Jane stood there, her anger dissipated to frost.

Karen stepped forward and got in the kid's face. 'Gary Wilkie, I'm arresting you for—'

'It wasn't me.'

'—the crime of murder.'

'It wasn't me!' Gary slapped her hands away. 'I wasn't there. It wasn't me in that taxi.'

'Gary, you need to stop lying to us.'

'I was here at home, playing games.'

'But you told us you were inv—'

'I wasn't.' Gary stood up and looked over at her, his hand spraying greasy hair back over his head. 'I'm just a part-timer. And I'm underage. They didn't invite me to the party.'

'So that stuff about you becoming a big shot?'

'It was...' He sighed. 'I've never spoken to anyone except my manager.'

'Gary, this all seems a bit far-fetched. Like you're trying to wriggle out of a murder charge.'

'I'm stressed, okay?'

'Stress is a very common experience with people who have killed, especially in cold blood. Especially when—'

'No.' Jane moved back, getting between them, but she was defending her son this time. 'You don't understand. Gary's been off school with stress. Last night, I drove him to see his therapist down in the Ferry.'

'It's also common for parents to lie to protect their children.'

'I'm not lying.' Jane was crying now. 'Gary's been off school for a month now. He just went back two weeks ago. But the stress was a lot to handle, so he needed to speak to his therapist again.' She rubbed her eyes. 'Carly and Teri. Those girls... Carly... I don't know how she did it, but she made him think he was her boyfriend, and she got him to send her a...' She clamped her eyes shut.

'What?' Vicky was clenching her fists tight. The motive was getting stronger and stronger. 'What did he send?'

'A dick pic!' Gary shouted it loud. 'I sent them a photo of my hard-on!'

Jane slumped back against the fridge, making the metal rattle. 'Carly and Teri shared it on social media, and not by accident either. They were cruel witches.'

'Given your son's age, that would actually be distributing child pornography.'

'Well, you should have a word with your colleagues.

The useless sods who didn't investigate it. Just said it was anonymous.'

Gary wrapped an arm around his mother. 'I thought Carly loved me, but she ruined my life.'

That all made perfect sense. Getting a kid to share a photo like that, shaming him. Ruining his life, or at least making him feel like it was ruined. Certainly enough to warrant an attack, if not outright murder.

'Did you speak to their parents?'

'I didn't have direct proof, did I? It was all anonymous, they'd been so careful, hadn't they? But Carly was the one who had the photo. She's responsible for it.'

'As painful as it is, Gary, you'll get over this. You're not the first and you won't be the last.'

'What would you know?'

Vicky stared hard at him. Nothing, except for a school trip when she was fourteen. Her boyfriend, or so she thought, photographing her breasts. A Polaroid shared with his friends. Nothing like the number of people as if it was on social media, but still. A lot of damage was done.

Vicky could've told them about her dad and a couple of his mates threatening to beat the living shit out of the boy, but she didn't. She got over it, but it still hurt. She had that acid bubbling in her stomach, like she was walking the halls of Carnoustie High School, with kids joking about her breasts.

Gary couldn't look at her.

Karen grabbed hold of him again. 'Come on, let's get you to the station.' She frogmarched the boy out of the kitchen into the hall.

Vicky stared at Jane. 'I know what you're going through, okay? It's going to be really tough for you. And I'm really sorry—'

Gary pushed his head towards Karen.

She was way too quick for him, ducking inside, then grabbing his throat and choking him against the wall. 'Come on!'

Jane shot after her son. 'Gary! No!'

Vicky followed outside, the cold air hitting her own burning cheeks.

'NO!' Jane was over by Karen, her resolve and calm given way to slapping and shouting. 'LET HIM GO!'

Karen opened the pool car's back door and dipped Gary's head to nudge him inside.

But he wouldn't go. He just stood there, resisting Karen's pushing, staring back at his mother.

Jane was looking between them. 'I can get his therapist here! I can get her on the phone!'

Gary collapsed to his knees, crying. 'I didn't do anything!'

'Please!' Jane was in Vicky's face. 'I can get her here. Will it help?'

'We'll need to speak to his counsellor as part of our investigation.'

'Please, don't do this. Let me have a Christmas with him.'

Vicky kept her arms out in case the mother tried to attack her. 'I suggest you call a lawyer.'

Jane let a gasp escape her lips. She looked back at the house. Her husband was standing in the doorway, clutching a whisky glass. 'Mike! Please! You've got to help!'

But Mike just sank the whisky and rested the glass on the side table by the door. He stared at his wife, close to hysteria now, then at his son, sobbing on the pavement, then shut his eyes. 'It was me. I killed her.'

17

L ike father like son.

Mike Wilkie leaned forward, breathing whisky-breath across the table. He was frozen, unable to move or to talk.

The interview room still reeked of Gary's earlier sickness – no amount of cleaning fluid could get rid of that so quickly.

His lawyer sat next to Mike. An overweight man, pushing towards obese. Tidy beard and close-cropped hair. He stood up and thrust out a hand that was bigger than Vicky's head. 'Jason Adamson of McLintock and Williams. Pleased to meet you.'

Vicky shook it with a smile. 'An Edinburgh firm, right?'

'Well, aye, but I'm a Dundee lad. Well, Monifieth. But I

live in Edinburgh now. Just got home for Christmas, and I was deep in a sleep in my old room, when I got the call from him upstairs. Campbell McLintock himself. And you don't bounce his call, let me tell you. You don't sleep through it.'

'Well, you were in the right place at the right time.'

'Indeed.' Adamson sat down and clicked his pen, ready to write on the yellow legal pad in front of him. His lips quivered, like he was stifling a yawn. 'I'm just here to make sure our client's confession is duly noted.' He gave in to the yawn now.

'Of course.' Vicky hoped that was the last exchange she'd have with him. But then again, she didn't believe the sudden flash of honesty from Mike Wilkie, especially with his son in cuffs by a police car, mid-arrest. 'I need you to go over your confession again, for the record.'

Mike nodded. 'You know why I did it. Why I killed Carly Johnston. I mean, it was an accident, but...' He sighed. 'But you know why, right?'

'It's important to get it on the record.'

'Okay.' Mike gripped his thighs, head forward, almost touching the desk. 'My son had shared a... a... a photo of his penis with Carly. It somehow ended up on Schoolbook and other social networks, shared among his supposed friends at school.'

'And you believe Carly was responsible.'

'Who else? My son deleted the image from his phone

and she was supposed to, but... but she didn't. Next thing I know, my son is crying about how it's ruined his life. And it did, at least for a while. He's only just recovering. All that therapy doesn't come cheap, and...'

'Did you report it to the police?'

'That's the trouble. They couldn't prove it was Carly who shared it. Or Teresa Ennis.'

And that made a modicum of sense. Still proved nothing either way. 'So why is that the trouble?'

'Because I know her father. Ryan.' Mike looked around the room. 'He's... he's... he's a police officer.'

'So you thought he'd use his contacts to keep a lid on it?'

'Stands to reason, doesn't it?'

'There are procedures in place for reporting police corruption.'

'Hmm.'

'I'm serious. If you think that "we investigate our own" and it's all covered up, well that's a very outdated view. We have officers from other divisions to investigate. If you had reported the matter to the authorities, a full and proper investigation would've occurred in the event of any corruption. Did you speak to Teresa's family?'

'My wife went into the local station, but she got stonewalled.'

'I see.'

Adamson sat back, mirroring his client's body

language. 'A shared dick pic is pretty common nowadays, though, right?'

Mike was blushing, eyes shut.

'What. Don't tell me—'

'My son has a very unusually shaped penis.' Mike shook his head. 'But the image was clearly of my son with... with... with his penis on display. And everyone at the school was going on about it. Calling him names. So, anyway, after my work night out yesterday, I—'

'Hold on a second.' Vicky raised a hand. '*You* had a night out?'

'Correct. I'm an accountant at Hunt and Ward in town. We usually have our night out at the start of the month, but places had booked up, so we could only get the twenty-third. Town was busy and they all went on to a nightclub, so I got a cab home.'

'When was this?'

'Just after midnight.'

Which tallied with Alan Kettles and his sneaky GPS tracker. 'Did you call for it?'

'No, it was from the rank at the Overgate.'

'You know the driver?'

'No.' Mike let his arms go, hanging by his side. 'But he seemed to know me. The friendly sort. Name of Dougie McLean.'

It hit Vicky like a sledgehammer. After tying up Catriona Gordon, McLean *had* gone back to work. Maybe

McLean was innocent of Carly's murder, but he had raped Catriona. And left her tied up. And eaten some beans on toast.

'This McLean chap started chatting to me in the cab, you know how it is. He was talking about snaring young lassies on an app. "Poggr. Without the e, ken." Right?' Mike's refined accent slipped to Dundonian for the fairly accurate impression. 'Then he told me that one of these "young lassies" lived nearby.'

'Where was this?'

'Near my home.'

'Adelaide Place?'

'Correct. And it was Carly. He described her as a "tidy piece" and said he'd been "banging her for over six months now, but had to break it off because she was too eager". I was still angry with Carly, but... When I asked for a receipt for the taxi, it irked McLean. He said he'd text me it. But I sensed he was up to something, so I insisted he do it there and then, sending me a receipt to my email. So he started to. And I saw that he didn't have a passcode on his phone. Schoolboy error. I realised that phone could be useful. So I made myself sick in the back of the car. And it certainly pissed him off. And cost me fifty pounds. But it allowed me to steal his phone. And I saw a plan. I could take the phone, see if he had photos of her on it. But there was nothing... Whatever McLean was doing to her was in person not on camera ... but it was too good of an opportunity to pass up. So I wanted to scare the life out of her and enact revenge for my son's ordeal.'

'By killing her?'

'God no. Just... Just kidnap her, take some nude photos and videos, then share them. Give her a taste of her own medicine. And if I could frame Douglas McLean for the crime? All the better.'

'Why frame him? What had he done?'

'Well, I initially wasn't going to, but when I found that app, Poggr, well. Let's just say that when Mr McLean said he found "young lassies" on there, he had a taste for *very* young.'

'How young?'

'Hard to say. I saw a girl who said she was 41, but she would never pass for that.'

Vicky felt her stomach go. She caught the same look of revulsion in Karen. Forty-one when she was fourteen. And Dougie McLean must've known. 'Go on.'

'Well, I wasn't there for that. But I found the messages he'd sent to Carly. A lot of them, until he broke it off with her by text. So I used it to snare her, promising that he'd made a mistake. And I arranged a meeting the following night, with the promise of a fancy hotel room. That place down where the V&A is going.'

'And she thought you were him?'

'Douglas had let her down. Dumped her, so it took a bit of persuading. And Carly was playing it cool. She said she was going to a party with her friend, Teresa, who was meeting her boyfriend who worked in Ashworth's afterwards. I suggested picking Carly up at the Ashworth's car park, and we could go to the hotel room I booked for some sexy fun. She agreed. Carly turned up, but Teresa had given her a lift there.' Mike smiled. 'I couldn't believe my luck. Both my son's tormentors in one place.'

'Wait a second. She'd know what car Mr McLean drove.'

'Correct. A silver Skoda Octavia, the one I'd seen dropping her off so many times.'

'Did you buy one?'

'Didn't have to.' Mike leaned forward again. 'Dougie called me on his phone. I pretended to be someone who had found it. I arranged to hand him the phone in the car park at the top of the Law, said I'd be driving a BMW 3-series.'

'And did you?'

'No. I waited for Dougie, for a lot longer than I expected, but he turned up. Then I had to wait for a young couple to leave. He phoned me back, and I said I'd been held up with work. But when the couple left, I went over.'

'Did he recognise you?'

'Didn't give him a chance. I knocked on the window and he started to get out. I wrapped my arms around him.' Mike enacted it on his lawyer, applying a sleeper hold. 'I've seen this in films and the wrestling on TV. I found a few videos on YouTube. It cuts off the flow of blood to the brain and knocks people out.'

'You did this to Mr McLean?'

'About half an hour before I was due to meet Carly. I tied him up in the bushes and drove off.'

This was all fitting together too well. Vicky didn't know whether his son had told him it all, but... But it felt more likely that Mike Wilkie had killed her.

'Then what?'

'I drove over to Ashworth's. Carly and Teresa weren't there, so I was relieved. Then I waited, and started to worry that I'd missed them. But I saw them approach, in that old thing Teresa was driving. I let them see the car, left it in a cone of light, then waited in the darkness. They drove up and got out. I pulled a knife and forced Teresa into the boot of the Skoda.'

'And Carly?'

'She resisted me. She wasn't going to run. I had her friend's life in my hands. But she grabbed my mask and pulled it free. She saw who it was. And she ran. I chased, but I fell over.'

'On her?'

'No. On the ice. The knife scattered. I lost it under a car. And she was shouting at me, calling me boomerang man's dad. Asking if I had the same deformed penis. Kicking me. And saying what he was wearing in the video.'

'The video?'

'She'd recorded my son on a video call. Got him to wear my wife's bra and pants. And I lost it. I grabbed her leg and pulled her over. She might've slipped on the ice, but she kept calling me "boomerang dad" and I lost it. I strangled her with my gloved hands. And she was dead.'

Vicky sat in the cool silence, just Adamson's pen making any sound. 'Then what?'

'What do you think? I panicked, of course. I drove off.'

'With Teresa in the boot.'

'Right. I'd forgotten about her. And I drove around the town, trying to figure out a plan. Then I got a call from you, Victoria, saying that my son was a suspect in Carly's murder. It all hit home. It was getting worse. You'd found her body. You'd linked my son to her. But you let him go when he told you about Dougie McLean, didn't you? So I drove him home, and left him with Jane. I told her I was going to have a word with Ryan Ennis.'

'You were trying to frame McLean for your crime.'

'He was a guilty man, so what was one more crime?'

Brutal.

'I found some videos on his phone. A young girl being raped. Screaming as he tied her up. Pleading. I realised I was dealing with someone who deserved what they were getting.'

'You should've handed that over to the police.'

'Well, I did the next best thing. I switched the phone

on and ran. My car was down the hill. I saw the blue lights as I got in and drove off. Listen, when I met him and he was asking for his phone back, I told him I'd found a website open, with that video, marked as Catriona. I got him to strip off, told him to stay there. Get in his car and phone back in two hours. And I came back. I drove them up to the Law. It was harder to knock him out than Teresa, but I put him in the car, sleeping, with Teresa in the boot, and I switched his phone on. I knew you'd find him quickly, or he'd wake up. So he was a guilty man. What harm was there in adding murder to it? It might help you secure his conviction.'

'But it wasn't him.'

'No. The guilt ate at me. I'd killed someone. A young girl, her whole life ahead of her. She'd wronged my son, but I'd taken her life. I was just trying to help my son.'

18

Dougie McLean looked tired, but was clearly trying to hide it with his usual bluster and confidence. Still, he wouldn't make eye contact with Vicky. 'Don't know what you're talking about.'

She sat back enough to make the chair creak. 'You do.'

'You seem to know a lot about my life.'

'I know about the three or so hours where you were knocked out and held in captivity naked at the monument.'

Now he made eye contact. 'Right.'

'Were you?'

'Maybe.' McLean stared up at the ceiling. 'I mean... Aye. I was attacked at the Law. And you woke us up there.

But...' He frowned. 'I woke up in the bushes, some boy was there. Asking me loads of questions.'

'About what?'

'This and that.'

'Come on. What was he asking?'

'Nothing much. Shite about Carly. About Teresa.'

'Did you see him?'

'Hardly. It was pitch black. He'd tied me up, so I couldn't move.'

'That's how you left Catriona Gordon.'

'Come on, you're still on about that?'

'Your fingerprints are all over the crime scene.'

'Keep telling you, that lassie had this fantasy about—'

'Don't.' Vicky's glare shut him down. 'It wasn't some sex game gone wrong. You *raped* her. And you left her tied up. You ate *beans on toast* in her kitchen. Then you collected another fare on the street. She would have died if we hadn't found her.'

McLean sat there, arms wrapped tight around his torso. 'What's my help worth?'

'It'll give you a clean conscience.'

McLean laughed.

'It'll help prosecute the man who attacked you. The man who stole your car, stole your phone, who knocked you out, tied you up and left you in the bushes.'

McLean exhaled slowly, then nodded fast. 'So what do you want to know?'

'Just anything about this place you were in.'

'Okay. Well, like I told you in my interview and you didn't believe me, I went to the Law, to meet the boy who'd nicked my phone. Right? Only, someone attacked me. Grabbed me from behind, wrapped his arms around my throat and the next thing I know, I wake up in the bushes.'

'Did you see anything that might—?'

'Pitch black, like I said. And my head was full of mince.'

Which backed up Mike Wilkie's story. 'You were very evasive about your location at the time of Carly's murder. And with Catriona's rape.'

McLean leaned forward, kneading his forehead like it was a loaf of bread. 'Christ. You're seriously doing me with her rape?'

'Yes. And you're going to go down for it. We've got it on video. To say nothing of the forty-one-year-old woman, who we have yet to identify but will no doubt turn out to be fourteen... Aye, we know about that too and it's only a matter of time before we have her signed up as well.'

McLean shook his head.

Vicky pushed her seat back and stood up. She leaned over to Karen. 'We're done here.' She walked over to the door and took one last look at the raping bastard. He was going to rot for a long time. Then she pushed out into the corridor. The stale air tasted like she was on a hike up in the glens with her dad.

Considine was lurking around.

'You still here?'

'Sarge, aye. Hate to see him get away with it.'

'He's not.' Vicky looked back at the door. 'In fact, can you take him downstairs and get him charged?'

'Sarge.' He slipped inside the room, brandishing his handcuffs.

Vicky checked her watch. Just after three, half an hour drive at this time, even with the ice. She'd get a few hours' sleep before Bella came clambering into her bed, hunting for presents. She smiled at Karen and caught her yawn. 'Time to get home. I'll see you in five minutes.'

'Vicks.' Karen walked off along the corridor.

Vicky opened the door to the Obs Suite.

Forrester was leaning on the back legs of his chair, his feet on the desk. Very precarious. The screen showed Considine trying to help McLean up, but he was staying rooted to the spot. 'Honestly, some people, eh?'

'Tell me about it.' Vicky stayed by the door. 'Considine is just taking McLean down to do him with Catriona's rape.'

'Well, that's a decent result, isn't it?' Forrester shook his head. 'Shame a girl's dead and another's in hospital because of— Jesus Christ!'

On the screen, Ennis was somehow in the interview room, aiming his fists over the lawyer's arms at Mike Wilkie's head.

Shit, shit, shit.

Vicky darted back down the corridor and tore open the door.

Considine lay on the floor, completely out of it.

The lawyer wasn't up to handling Ryan Ennis, just took one sock to the jaw and he went down.

Then Ennis had Mike in a headlock. 'Think you can do that to my daughter, do you?'

'Ryan!'

Ennis looked over at Vicky. 'What, you're going to save this piece of shit?'

'Don't.'

'Bugger this!' Ennis pushed Mike against the wall. One punch to his throat, a second to his gut, then he went down. Ennis launched a kick at his face, then put his foot on his neck.

Vicky grabbed Ennis by the arm, but caught a flailing hand in the face. His wedding ring took a chunk out of her lip.

Sod this.

Vicky launched herself shoulder first at Ennis, pushing him away from Mike and pinning him against the wall. Another of her dad's old tricks came out to play – she drove the crown of her head right into his nose. Less a Glasgow kiss, more a Dundonian handshake.

Ennis was squealing. She pushed him down on the

floor, and reached for Considine's cuffs lying in the middle of the floor.

'You coward.' Ennis's voice was muffled. 'You absolute coward.'

But Mike Wilkie wasn't in any shape to hear. Eyes shut, mouth hanging loose.

Forrester was in the doorway. He let the duty doctor past him. 'Christ, tell me he's alive.'

19

Vicky was on her feet, stomping around Forrester's office, mobile in her hand, just waiting to give him the news.

Forrester put his desk phone down and slurped coffee out of his mug. World's Best Father. Not a dad, but a father. 'Well.'

'That's it? That's all you're going to say?'

'What, you want me to say we're charging Ennis?'

'Aye, I do. He attempted to murder a suspect. He deserves jail time for this. At the very least, he should be kicked off the force.'

Forrester took a slow sip of coffee. 'Come on, Doddsy, after all you've been through with him.'

'We've been through *nothing*.'

'That's bollocks. He turned you from a rough-and-ready DC into the DS you are today.'

'No he didn't!'

'Aye, he did. Course he did.'

'Sir, that is absolute bollocks and you know it.'

Forrester kept his peace.

Vicky leaned against his desk. 'So, what, you're going to try and cover it up?'

'Maybe.'

'That's corruption.'

Forrester flicked his wrist towards the door. 'None of that was recorded. It's just the word of Mike Wilkie and that lawyer against us.'

'No.'

'Come on, Vicky. Ryan's a good cop. He's got a good conviction rate. That guy put his daughter in the boot of a car and...'

'I sympathise with his situation, really I do. Convicting Wilkie for Ennis's daughter's ordeal is the right thing to do. Hospitalising him isn't.'

Forrester finished his coffee and put the mug back on the desk, nudging it away. 'Any word?'

'On who? Wilkie?'

'Teresa.'

'She's going to be okay. Physically. Psychologically, the doctor is less sure. But Wilkie's in a coma.'

'He's what?' Forrester's eyes were wide. 'A *coma*?'

'No, he's not.' Vicky rolled her eyes at him. 'But he's not speaking to us, is he? He might've killed someone, but he's a victim too.'

Forrester sighed. 'Had me going. Guy like that, he had no idea what he was doing. Stands to reason he'd go all catatonic. I mean...' But he trailed off.

'You need to report this higher, sir. You need to call this into DCS Soutar.'

'I can't, Vicky.'

'Why, because you and Ennis go back years?'

'Loyalty is earned.'

'He's—'

'Vicky, you think a guy like me, from my day and age, gets where he is by colouring inside the lines all the time? I made some *compromises*, and Ennis knows most of them. He goes down, I go down. Is that what you want?'

Vicky knew she wasn't going to persuade him by fighting him. 'So what's the plan, then?'

'We'll get him home tonight. Let him sleep a night in his bed. I'll call Soutar, like you say.'

'On Christmas Day?'

'No. Christ, no. I'll wait until Monday. Meantime, Ryan can get into the doctor's, get a sick note, get him to sign him off long term. Mental stress, something like that, no longer fit for duty due the rigours he's endured.'

'You're a coward.' As much as Vicky wanted to say that, she kept her own peace. Just let him spill out his plan.

'I'm a survivor, Doddsy. Before I speak to Soutar, I'll put in a word with some contacts. Won't be Grampian or Highlands who investigate, but I've got some mates in the old Lothian & Borders and the old Strathclyde, they're the ones likeliest to investigate him.' He sat forward, running his hands through his hair. 'Was thinking that maybe we can give Considine credit for McLean's arrest. Give him credit for catching him for Catriona Gordon's rape.'

'So you can throw the press a bone?'

'Aye. Keep them off the scent.'

'Surprised you're not going to frame McLean for the murders.'

'Full confession, Doddsy. I'll take that. And Ennis was nowhere near the case.'

'Right.'

'Tell me I'm doing the wrong thing here.'

Vicky held his gaze. 'You know you are.'

'Look, it's a man thing. Okay?'

'A *man* thing?'

'Aye. Ry wants to protect his kid. Maybe you wouldn't do the same—'

'Don't.'

'See? You don't understand.'

Vicky felt that twanging pain in the back of her neck.

Like she was going to snap. She got up to standing again. 'See you on Monday, sir. Have a good Christmas.' She walked over to the door.

'Seriously, not a word of this to anyone.'

Vicky stood there, head bowed. 'I'll see.'

20

Vicky put her key in the lock and eased the door open. She stopped on the threshold and listened as she removed her key. Letting heat out, but trying to listen for who was still up.

A strange clacking sound.

What the hell?

She stepped inside and nudged the door behind her, then raised the handle to lock it. It didn't click too loudly. She stepped around the side of the creaky floorboard and traced the clacking to the living room.

Mum was sitting on the sofa, mouthing some secret incantation as she knitted away.

That explained it, then.

Vicky felt her tension release. All through her shoulders and neck. She stepped over to the door, opened it and pushed it shut.

'Is that you, Victoria?'

Tinkle was lying on her lap, the cat all curled up. And Mum looked terrified of her.

Vicky eased off her jacket and hung it up. 'Aye, it's me.'

Dad lay supine on the armchair, legs fully extended. His headphones lay on his belly. He opened his mouth and let out the rawest snore.

Vicky dumped her coat on the side table and leaned in to kiss her mother. 'You okay?'

'I was shattered, but I had a good sleep while we were waiting.'

'Thanks, Mum.' Vicky carefully extricated Tinkle from her lap and set her down on the actual cat bed. 'Has his snoring done any structural damage, do you know?'

'I wouldn't be surprised.' Mum started putting her knitting away. 'We'll get out of your hair, then.'

'I'll drive you home.'

'Not with the wee one upstairs.'

Vicky blushed. 'Right, no.'

'And the walk will do us good.' Mum pushed herself up to standing. Looked painful. 'George!'

'What's that?' He licked his lips a few times.

'Wake up!'

'Just resting my eyes.'

'George, we're going home.'

He shifted round. 'I'll stay here.'

'No, you won't.' Mum walked over and prodded a knitting needle into his side.

He yelped and jerked up. 'What are you doing?'

'Get up. Victoria needs to get on.'

'Right.' He rubbed at his eyes, then looked at his daughter. 'Hey.'

'I'll just get his beer out of the fridge, then we'll be gone.' Mum scuttled off out of the room.

He looked over at Vicky. Didn't seem to be in any hurry to get up. 'You catch him?'

'Them.'

'One of those?'

'Complex, aye.'

'Want to talk about it?'

Vicky glanced over at the door. Sounded like Mum was clearing out half of the fridge. Or loading it with stuff she shouldn't. Chocolates, cakes, chocolate cake. 'You ever work with Ryan Ennis?'

'Oh aye. What did we call him?' Dad clicked his fingers. 'That's it. The Rube.'

'What's a rube?'

'It's an American thing. A country bumpkin. Easily fooled and parted from their money by big city types. Kid was daft as a brush. One time, Davie Forrester got him to guard a coat hanger and a jacket. For twelve hours! Didn't even look to see if it was a bloke sitting there. Thought he was just the silent type.'

Vicky flashed up her eyebrows. 'So he goes back a ways with Forrester?'

'Long time. Davie was one of my DCs, then we got The Rube in as a Training DC. Why do you ask?'

'It's a long story.'

'You want to tell me now?'

'Dad, someone kidnapped Ryan's daughter. He beat the living shit out of the guy. And I mean, absolutely battered him. He's in hospital.'

'I see. You remember that wee shite, Craig Norrie? What he did to you?'

'Aye, I remember. And I remember what you did to him.'

'I didn't really do anything.'

'But he didn't do it again.'

'Exactly.'

'This is different, Dad.'

'Is it? The things I did to protect you. It's not any different.'

Vicky wanted to argue, but she was so bloody tired. She collapsed onto the sofa, roasting from where Mum had been sitting, and stroked Tinkle's soft fur. 'So I shouldn't report him?'

'Depends what Forrester's asking you to do.'

'Sounds like he'll fudge any investigation into Ryan.

Get someone connected to him to park the inquiry. Or maybe not even start one.'

'I see.'

Mum battered into the room, loaded down with a couple of big bags. 'Right, George. Let's get along the road.'

'Okay-doke.' Dad hefted himself up to standing. 'Well, we'll see you and that ball of mischief in the morning.' He leaned in to kiss Vicky, but whispered, 'Go easy on Ryan. Please. And trust Davie. You've got a foot in both camps, Vicky. Don't forget your past.' He paused. 'Or mine.'

Vicky nodded. 'I'll think about it.'

Mum handed Dad both bags. 'Come on, then. I'll have to get the turkey on at six, so it's not like I'll get much sleep.'

'You slept for Scotland earlier, dear.' Dad followed her out of the room.

Vicky got up and walked out into the hallway. 'Thanks for babysitting. Lifesavers.'

'Don't mention it. It was a real pleasure.' Mum stepped out into the night. 'Christ, it's freezing.'

Vicky shut the door and listened to them arguing their way up the road until all she could hear was the occasional passing car up on the Barry Road.

What the hell was she going to do about Ennis?

Play along with Forrester's game?

Did she have the option of going against him?

She just didn't know.

But that was for another day.

Now, she had more important things to worry about. She crept up the stairs, taking it really slowly.

Bella was in her bed, tucked in nice and tight. She made a cute chuckling sound in her sleep.

Vicky went into her own bedroom and unlocked the cupboard. Bella's stocking was lying there, already stuffed full of presents. She grabbed it, just as her phone chimed.

Probably Forrester seeing the error of his ways. Or Mum had left something in the fridge.

Christ.

She put down the stocking and checked the message. She almost dropped the phone. Almost threw it against the wall.

It was from Alan:

Hey, Vicks. Long time no speak. Just having a few with the boys and was wondering how you were doing? A

Vicky clutched the stocking, tight in her hand. Bella's father, just texting her out of the blue like that. Didn't seem like he had any idea, though.

She needed to keep it that way.

Vicky pressed the button to block his number, then sneaked through to Bella's room.

READY FOR MORE?

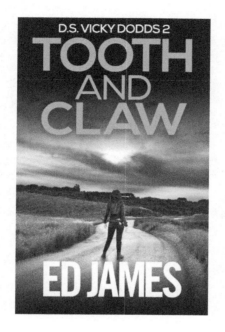

Out now, buy on Amazon

The next book in the series, TOOTH AND CLAW, is out now — keep reading to the end of this book for a sneak preview. You can get a copy at Amazon.

Note that I've replaced the opening chapter with a new one that is a lot less shocking.

If you would like to be kept up to date with my new releases, please join the Ed James Readers Club at geni.us/EJmailer.

AFTERWORD

Huge thanks for buying and reading this book. I hope you enjoyed it.

This series has been a labour of love for me. Vicky Dodds lives in the town I grew up in (as much as a 42-year-old manchild can grow up, eh?) and covers the city I used to visit every weekend for record shops, cinemas and, later, pubs and clubs. I hope I captured some of Dundee's gritty and unique character — while it's much-maligned and the butt of a lot of jokes in Scotland, I do really like the place. It's got a very distinct history and some proud people.

And it didn't start as a series. In 2014, my first year as a full-time author, the first novel I wrote was SNARED, which I thought would become a new series, after the existing five Cullen books. Amazon's Thomas & Mercer graciously published it, way more successfully than I could have myself, and through various deals for the DI Fenchurch books, we discussed a sequel, which always got pushed out in favour of another Fenchurch. They reverted the rights to SNARED in 2018 and I heavily edited it and republished it as TOOTH & CLAW. Then I wrote another two books in the series, FLESH & BLOOD and the forthcoming SKIN & BONE, out on the 1st May 2021. And all that time, I had an idea to do this prequel, fleshing out a couple of lines in TOOTH & CLAW, about how Considine caught a taxi driver and what happened to DS Ennis. I hope it was worth the effort!

Thanks to Allan and Vicki for editing work this time out.

One final thing, if you liked this, then please leave a review on Amazon — it really helps aspiring indie authors like me.

Thanks for reading it.

— Ed James,
Scottish Borders, March 2021

OTHER BOOKS BY ED JAMES

SCOTT CULLEN MYSTERIES SERIES

Eight novels featuring a detective eager to climb the career ladder, covering Edinburgh and its surrounding counties, and further across Scotland.

1. GHOST IN THE MACHINE
2. DEVIL IN THE DETAIL
3. FIRE IN THE BLOOD
4. STAB IN THE DARK
5. COPS & ROBBERS
6. LIARS & THIEVES
7. COWBOYS & INDIANS
8. HEROES & VILLAINS

CULLEN & BAIN SERIES

Six novellas spinning off from the main Cullen series covering the events of the global pandemic in 2020.

1. CITY OF THE DEAD
2. WORLD'S END
3. HELL'S KITCHEN
4. GORE GLEN

5. DEAD IN THE WATER
6. THE LAST DROP

CRAIG HUNTER SERIES

A spin-off series from the Cullen series, with Hunter first featuring in the fifth book, starring an ex-squaddie cop struggling with PTSD, investigating crimes in Scotland and further afield.

1. MISSING
2. HUNTED
3. THE BLACK ISLE

DS VICKY DODDS SERIES

Gritty crime novels set in Dundee and Tayside, featuring a DS juggling being a cop and a single mother.

1. BLOOD & GUTS
2. TOOTH & CLAW
3. FLESH & BLOOD
4. SKIN & BONE

DI SIMON FENCHURCH SERIES

Set in East London, will Fenchurch ever find what happened to his daughter, missing for the last ten years?

Other Books

Other crime novels, with Senseless set in southern England, and the other three set in Seattle, Washington.

TOOTH AND CLAW
PROLOGUE

'I see.' Rachel gripped her mobile as tight as she could without cracking the screen. 'I'm sorry you see it that way.'

Benji was tugging at his lead, desperate to sniff at the lamp post over the road. Little sod might be small for a pug, but he was strong.

Up here, she got a great view down to the Tay, shimmering in the spring sunshine. A boat was cutting up surf on its way out to sea, heading for the two bridges across the river. The honeysuckle was starting to send out its sickly sweet perfume, as sure a sign as any that summer was coming.

'Listen, you just give us the money back and we'll say no more.' His voice was harsh, distorted by her phone's speakers. 'I'm not an angry or vindictive man. That's all.'

Rachel let Benji have his way and crossed the road. 'Well, I'm afraid I can't just—'

'Listen, you sold us a pup!'

'Literally. We agreed the terms. Now goodbye!' Rachel ended the phone call and scanned through her contacts list for the man's number. Before she could block him, he was calling her back. How rude! She killed the call, then tapped the button to block him. Excellent. A wave of calm surged through her. 'Come on, Benji.' She tugged at his lead and set off down the grass verge on this side of the lane, uneven but preferable to walking on the road.

That woman was staring hard at her over the fence. It hadn't been here a week ago, but now its varnished wood barred any view of the garden. Used to be one of the highlights of Rachel's day, but now it was... Well. 'Don't you even *think* of letting those dogs get in here again.'

Rachel shook her head. Some people just didn't get it, did they?

'I'm talking to you!' She was keeping pace with Rachel and shooting angry looks over the fence. 'Your bloody dogs should be—'

'I'm not listening to you.' Rachel tightened her grip, quickened her pace, but held her keys in her pockets in case she needed a weapon.

'Snooty cow. You and your horrible little—'

'Snooty?' Rachel chanced a look at the spiteful woman. 'If you knew half of—'

'Yeah, yeah, yeah. Just keep walking. And don't come back.'

'Gladly.' Rachel spotted that point where the pavement picked up across the road. One last look over the fence, though. 'Good day to you.'

'Good day? *Good day?* Christ! I've lost a year thanks to you!'

Rachel jogged over the road away from the harpy.

A car horn jolted her out of her rage.

Some black thing was stopped in the middle of the road. The driver was shouting something at Rachel, but the glass muted whatever it was.

'Come on, you too.' Rachel clutched the leads in both hands and dragged Benji and Jemima across the road.

'Could say thanks for not running you over!' A woman's voice, soon drowned out by the roar of the car's engine and the bitter tang of burnt petrol.

What was wrong with people?

Rachel hurried on down the pavement, eager to get away and get home in time for *Pointless.* Not too far now – she could see the back of their house off in the distance, behind the runs that filled their garden. If only there was a shortcut.

'Excuse me?' A car was coming up from behind, some dance music thumping out into the country air.

Rachel stopped, sighed, then made to turn.

Before she could, something hard pressed into her

back and it felt like her whole body shook and turned to jelly. She fell forward, unable to break her fall, and landed flat on the tarmac. Her cheek scraped off some loose stones.

The dogs looked back at her, then up at someone, then turned tail and ran away, their leads trailing behind them.

That was the last thing Rachel saw before something was shoved over her head.

You can buy TOOTH & CLAW now at Amazon.

If you'd like to be join my Readers Club and keep up to date on my new releases and get free exclusive content, please join for free at https://geni.us/EJmailer

Made in the USA
Las Vegas, NV
07 March 2024

86823060R00115